This was Nathan [barcode] **kissing.**

Not any old kiss either, but something that turned Molly on and made her knees weak and her heart rate go off the scale. She should stop, pull away.

She didn't want to. Couldn't. It was as though they'd been building toward this moment once they'd found themselves sitting together at breakfast yesterday. It was like being stuck in the path of a tornado with nowhere to hide. Not that she wanted to. So much for not trusting people. Except, not once had Nathan made her think he'd ever hurt her.

This was starting over, getting on with a new life, and if it involved getting closer to a man then she had to take the chance. Everything might have been on hold, but now the barriers were falling fast, not one at a time as she'd expected, but crashing at her feet in a pile. Leaning closer, she increased the pressure of her mouth on his and went with the wonderful moment, let the exquisite sensations his kiss created have their way and tease her with yearnings long forgotten.

Dear Reader,

Thank you for picking up my book. I hope you get as much enjoyment reading it as I did writing it.

Sydney was the first overseas city I ever visited, and I've returned often over the years. Fortunately my husband enjoys it as much as I do. So when I was thinking about where to set this story Sydney kept nudging and here we are.

When nurse Molly O'Keefe first dropped into my mind with a sad story I had to think about just who the man could be to rescue her from her past and lead her into a happy future. ER doctor Nathan Lupton has also faced a tragic past, which has made him very understanding of other people's needs, and he's perfect for Molly. If only they can both see that.

Follow these two through the highs and lows of falling in love and overcoming the past.

Cheers,

Sue MacKay

suemackayauthor@gmail.com
SueMacKay.co.nz

THE NURSE'S TWIN SURPRISE

———

SUE MacKAY

Recycling programs
for this product may
not exist in your area.

ISBN-13: 978-1-335-14917-6

The Nurse's Twin Surprise

First North American Publication 2019

Copyright © 2019 by Sue MacKay

Printed in U.S.A.

Books by Sue MacKay

Harlequin Medical Romance

SOS Docs
Redeeming Her Brooding Surgeon
The Ultimate Christmas Gift
Her New Year Baby Surprise

Midwife…to Mom!
Reunited…in Paris!
A December to Remember
Breaking All Their Rules
Dr. White's Baby Wish
The Army Doc's Baby Bombshell
Resisting Her Army Doc Rival
Pregnant with the Boss's Baby
Falling for Her Fake Fiancé
Baby Miracle in the ER
Surprise Twins for the Surgeon
ER Doc's Forever Gift
The Italian Surgeon's Secret Baby
Taking a Chance on the Single Dad

Visit the Author Profile page
at Harlequin.com for more titles.

**Praise for
Sue MacKay**

"Ms. MacKay has penned a delightful novel in this book where there were moments where I smiled and moments where I wanted to cry."

—*Harlequin Junkie* on
Resisting Her Army Doc Rival

CHAPTER ONE

FAKE IT TILL you make it.

Yes, sure. So easy. She did it all the time.

Try harder. Remember yesterday's courier delivery.

The final lock had been undone. She was free. Single again. Two years of waiting for the legal process to finally be over. Today was the first day of the rest of her life, and it was going to be a doozy.

That was once she worked out how to proceed with a newer, wiser, not so damned cautious version of herself that yesterday's delivery must shut the door on. Those baby steps she'd been making were fine, but the time had come to stride out, head high, wearing a 'don't mess with me' attitude. Starting now.

Molly O'Keefe pasted on a facsimile of a smile and turned to glare into Mr Nathan Lupton's eyes. And gasped. Those burnt-coffee eyes were spitting tacks. At her?

'What's wrong?'

That's your idea of don't mess with me? Try again.

'That phone call. Something I need to know?'

'I've just spent valuable time ringing round to put specialists on alert at five-thirty in the morning for a patient who's now been taken to another ED.' His hands gripped his hips.

'The man found lying by the train tracks?' Surely not even he was blaming *her*? They weren't friends, but this was ridiculous. The thumping starting up in her chest was deafening. No, he wouldn't be, but he was angry.

Not at me. I can handle this.

Really?

Absolutely. *Fake it till—*

Yeah, yeah, she knew that line back to front. Still needed some practice, that was all. Beginning right now.

'I wonder why the ambulance was redirected to another hospital when we're closest.'

Nathan was staring at her, though she wasn't certain he was actually seeing her. 'That's something I intend finding out. It's not happening again.' He was still angry. Who could blame him when they'd been flat out busy when the initial call had come through? So much for the patients tapering off in the early hours. 'Shouldn't you be keeping an eye on Archie Banks?' he barked.

Odd how on her first day in Sydney General's emergency department when he'd growled at her to get the defib, which she'd already been in the process of wheeling towards the Resus unit, she hadn't been afraid of him. Mightn't like him much, though to be fair she didn't know him except as a doctor, but she was never on guard around him or ever felt threatened by his grumpiness. Which said a lot. She'd think about that later. Right now an answer was required to placate him, because placating kept everyone happy—except maybe her—but it was an old habit she'd still not managed to dump. *Game face, girl.* Duh. Two seconds and her promise to herself had flown the coop.

'I was coming to see if you'd take another look at him. His pain level is increasing, not decreasing.' Nathan had administered a strong dose of painkiller forty minutes ago.

The anger softened. Of course it did. From what she'd seen around here Nathan adored children. 'Anything from the lab yet?'

'No, and I've only just checked,' she added hastily, raising one of her grandmother's glares in case he found fault with her. Another sign she might be getting her act together.

Dark eyebrows rose in that annoying manner of his that inexplicably riled her beyond reason. Then he swallowed and pulled up a smile.

'Sorry. It wasn't your fault the man was taken elsewhere after I've been chasing my tail preparing for his arrival.'

It wasn't the greatest of apologies, but he had tried, and that was unexpected. 'No problem.' None he need know about. She had a list of them, but nothing to do with work. This was her safe place. 'Archie?'

'On my way.' He strode off, his back ramrod straight, his jaw jutting out, yet she'd swear some of his tension had eased.

'Good girl, not letting him rile you.' Vicki nudged her, and brought her back to focusing on anything other than *Mr* Lupton.

'You think?' she asked around a tight laugh, her eyes still taking in the sight of Nathan despite trying to concentrate on what Vicki had to say.

'I do.' Her fellow nurse was also watching Nathan, now heading into a cubicle, and there was a thoughtful tone to her next question that unsettled Molly. 'Still coming to breakfast?'

'Wouldn't miss it for anything.' She meant every word, even after struggling with a strong reluctance to socialise and get too comfortable when she half expected to be nudged out of the way by people who wanted more from her than she was prepared to share. She had initially hesitated about accepting the invitation, then decided to give it a go. After all, Vicki had been friendly and helpful since she'd begun working in here two months ago.

A flicker of excitement warmed her. Look where *faking it* got her. Right into the middle of her colleagues, whose good intentions had brought her close to tears on occasion, even when she didn't trust them enough to give back anything of herself. Getting out and about with this crowd might go some way to fixing the loneliness that filled her days and nights. Not being a team player had come at a price, one that needed to be dealt with if she was to be happy again.

'Molly? Can you come here, please?' Nathan had reappeared in the cubicle doorway, back to being calm and efficient.

Molly looked at the man and, hiding the uncertainty he created in her belly, nodded. 'Need the phlebotomy kit?' Her voice had returned to non-confrontational, Gran's glare long gone. Situation normal. Previous normal. Lifting her shoulders, she reached for the bag of needles and tubes.

Nathan's smile might be reluctant, but it actually seemed genuine. Meaning it was further unsettling. 'Yes. I want liver functions done while we wait for the orderly to collect him.'

The boy, recovering from an appendicectomy last week, was back with pains in his gut and chest. Nathan suspected septicaemia and had started him on an array of intravenous antibiotics. They were now waiting for the children's ward to collect him.

In the cubicle, she said, 'Hey, Archie, I'm going to find you some dry pyjamas after I've cleaned you up.' With the fever drenching him continually, the boy needed regular wiping down.

Archie was eyeing the kit with trepidation. No hiding what was coming from this kid. 'I don't want another needle.'

'It's annoying, isn't it?' Nathan said as he slid the tourniquet up the boy's thin arm. 'You'll be able to tell all your friends how brave you are.'

Molly sponged Archie's legs, in an attempt to distract him. 'I hope you're not ticklish.' Not that she intended tickling him when Nathan was about to slide a needle into a vein. That would be taking distraction to the next level.

'Mum tickles me.' Archie's eyes were on Nathan, apprehension blinking out of his big eyes.

'There, all done.' Moments later Nathan handed her the tube of blood to name and date. 'Mark it urgent.'

'Right.' She headed for the hub to call for an orderly to take the blood sample to the lab.

Nathan had followed her. 'How're you settling in with us?'

'Fine.' I hope. 'I really like the job, and the people I work with.' Had she done something wrong he was about to mention? Wasn't she good enough at her work? The usual worry over making herself stand out began chugging through her mind.

'Good. We don't like swapping staff too often.' Then, 'So what do you do when you're not here?' Nathan was being friendly? Abnormally friendly, since he wasn't known for idle chitchat.

How to answer without giving herself away? 'There's always heaps of things needing attention where I live and people to check up on and shopping at the mall.' Drivel spilled over her lips. 'And I like going for walks.' Definitely faking it. She rarely left the apartment other than to come to work.

He was regarding her like he was sorry he'd asked. Good, then he wouldn't find any more questions for her. *Wrong.* 'Sounds like your evenings are free so you'll have time to come to our midwinter Christmas barbecue.' Nathan was talking about the out of season party some Aussies celebrated that had come about because of English people living in Australia who missed a cold Christmas. He tapped a sheet of paper lying on the desk. 'I don't see your name here.'

That was because she had no intention of

going. She wasn't ready for that level of integration. An hour over breakfast was one thing, a full-on party quite another. *Thought I was starting over, now that I'm free.* 'I haven't thought about it.' What excuse could she come up with? She tried to read the shift roster behind Nathan, but he was blocking her line of vision.

'It's a fortnight away but I like to know who's coming well in advance. Bring a plate and your own alcohol. Meat provided.' He was pointing a pen over his shoulder. 'You're not working that night.'

There went that excuse for not going. Little did he know about how hard it was for her to go anywhere that was attended by lots of people.

He hadn't finished. 'I encourage all the staff to join in. It's good for morale, amongst other things.'

New beginnings, remember? Deep breath. Go for it. Taking the pen from his fingers, mindful of not touching him, Molly scrawled her name beneath Vicki's and added *Dessert* next to it. 'There. Done.' And she hadn't stopped too long to think about it. *Definitely* a first.

'Good.' His tone didn't back his reply. Those toast-coloured eyes were focused on her as though she was a mystery he was trying to unravel. She'd probably surprised him by giving in so quickly when it was well known she didn't go out with any of the staff to movies or breakfasts.

Amazed at how easily she'd signed up, she stood absorbing the slow wave of excitement rolling through her. She could do this. She really, really could. 'Where's the barbecue being held?'

'At my place out in Coogee.' He picked up a patient file and began reading the notes. Dark blond hair fell over his brow, making her itch to push it back in place.

'Oh.' The heavy pounding in her chest had returned, and her mouth began drying up like an overbaked sponge. Why hadn't she noticed before that Nathan was disgustingly good looking? Probably her massive hang-up about getting close to men had kept the blinkers on until today, when she'd made the promise to move on, get a life. Did that mean finding love? Thump, thump, thump. It couldn't. That'd be going too far, too soon. Molly had learned Paul's lessons well. An absolute charmer, he'd sworn his undying love for her and wooed her completely. One year into their marriage the real Paul had come to light when he'd started hitting her whenever she'd disagreed with him, which was a sure-fire way of making her keep her mouth shut. Suddenly noticing Nathan as more than a doctor was scary. Wasn't it?

'Problem with that?' Nathan asked without looking up.

'Hell, yes.' She wasn't ready. It was too soon—wasn't part of the plan to move on.

Puzzlement blinked out at her. 'Why? It's usual to go to someone's house for a party.'

Embarrassment rose. She'd answered her question to herself out loud. This man was rattling her, which made no sense when, because of his self-assurance, she'd pretty much ignored him in the two months she'd worked here, unless it was to discuss a patient or argue over small things, like where the order for more syringes had got to. It'd been years since desire had lit her up, but if this tightness in her stomach and heat in her veins were any indication, she might be making up for lost time right now, in the middle of the ED. 'Um, of course. I didn't mean that. It's fine. I'll be there.'

The alarm sounded. Code one. Relief had her racing to Resus and the man sprawled on the floor, unconscious.

'Cardiac arrest,' Vicki said, her clasped hands pushing down regularly on the exposed chest.

Molly grabbed the electro pads, handed them to Nathan, who was right behind her. Next she snatched up the ventilator in preparation of a good outcome before kneeling down next to him.

'Fill us in on the details,' Nathan said as he prepared to administer a shock.

'Geoff Baxter, forty-eight, chest pains, readings show a minor cardiac arrest an hour ago,' Vicki intoned. 'He was getting stroppy and didn't want to stay on the bed. Started getting up and collapsed on the floor.'

'Clear.'

On Nathan's command everyone moved away from the patient. The lifeless body jerked. The line on the monitor remained flat. Vicki started back on the compressions and Molly squeezed the oxygen bottle when she reached thirty.

'Clear.' Nathan gave a second shock.

The line blipped, rose, then fell into an erratic pattern.

'That's better,' Molly nodded. 'Not perfect, but we're getting there.' She put the ventilator aside and got up to get the scoop stretcher so they could lift the man off the floor and back onto the bed.

Another nurse, Hank, attached an oxygen mask, then began wiping a bleeding abrasion on Geoff's forehead. 'He hit the floor hard.'

Nathan leaned close to the man. 'Geoff, can you hear me?'

Geoff opened his eyes briefly.

'You've had a cardiac arrest. We're going to

keep you in here for a while, then you'll be admitted to the intensive care unit.'

Geoff shook his head once. 'No.'

'That'll be a yes, then.' Nathan gave one of his megawatt smiles.

Molly's stomach stirred, and he hadn't even been looking in her direction. He'd often smiled at her, particularly whenever he'd wanted something unpleasant dealt with, but not in that full-on, cramp-her-stomach way he saved for others. Not that she'd given him reason to. Unless working hard and caring deeply about their patients counted, and apparently it didn't. That was expected of her, no reward given—or required.

Would a man ever again look at her and think, *She's lovely*? One without hard fists? Did she want a man to notice her, get to know her? This new idea had to be part of moving forward, didn't it? It was funny how in a previous, happy-go-lucky life she'd had her pick of gorgeous men, never had a problem finding a date for the glamorous occasions that came with being her entrepreneurial mother's daughter. Not funny, really. Glancing over her shoulder, she saw no one to frighten her. Not that she expected to, but there were still times she just had to check, even though Paul would be in jail for many years to come. She'd lost a lot, but she was free.

Hold on to that. And, yes, think about maybe one day falling love.

Vicki nudged her. 'Time to knock off, day shift's here.'

Another night done and survived without too much drama amongst the patients. She could relax, except her muscles weren't playing the game. The old tension tightened her stomach and neck, while her shoulder blades tried to meet in the middle of her back. Because of the past? Or did she put this down to the rare heat in her veins, stirred up by Nathan Lupton? Yeah, like that'd be a blast. *It might be.* As if. He'd have to get a lot friendlier first, though he had made an effort earlier. Were things looking up all round? Smiling at Vicki, she asked, 'Which shoes are you wearing this morning?'

'Those orange, thin-strapped ones you were green about last week.' Vicki was a shoeaholic, with an incredible collection that made Molly envious—and that was only over the shoes she'd seen at work.

Molly laughed. Twice in one morning? *Go for it.* 'Clothes are my go to when the urge to have some R and R in the malls beckons. Shoes always come second. Maybe I should try the shoe shops first next time because those ones are amazing. When you're sick of them you know which locker's mine,' she said. 'Let's go change.'

As well as her trousers and blouse, she needed to put her game face on.

Nathan turned from the specialist taking over Geoff's case. 'You all right?'

'Why wouldn't I be?' There were a million reasons, but he knew none of them, and never would.

'Because you look ready to bolt.'

Make that one million minus one reasons. Except this morning that had been the last thing on her mind. Disconcerting. She'd been laughing and he'd thought that? She hated that nearly as much as she'd hate him to see the truth. 'Actually, I'm working on how to nab Vicki's shoes without her noticing.'

His expression softened. 'Good luck with that.'

'I reckon.' Unbelievable. They were having a normal conversation for once.

'By the way, you were good with Geoff.'

Surprise stole the retort off her tongue. She hadn't done anything out of the ordinary, and yet he was saying that in front of the other nurses? She looked around at Vicki, then Hank, before locking eyes back on Nathan.

He got the message fast. 'So were you two.' He nodded. 'Right, get out of here while you can.' This time he was talking directly to Vicki.

Molly knew she could relax now that Nathan

was no longer focused on her, but it wasn't happening. Instead her body was winding up tighter than a ball of twine, and just as rough. Why did this man in particular make her feel a little lighter in the chest, as though hope was knocking? Hope for love one day? Sadly, never for family. That dream had been smothered as a wet sack would a flame by a fist in her belly that had stolen her baby and quite likely any chance of another.

She looked at Nathan as he laughed with Vicki over something, and her heart dropped. If only she had the courage to let a strong, confident man close enough to trust. Until now it never occurred to her to want the things Paul had stolen. But it couldn't be this man waking her up. They were mostly civil with each other, but it took more than civility for a relationship to succeed. Or maybe it didn't. There hadn't been any of that going on in her now defunct marriage.

Flip-flop went her heart. Her stomach softened as the tension started backing off. As though her body was telling her it was ready to have fun. Had certain parts of her anatomy forgotten the pain of the past? It wasn't wise. Or safe. But very tempting. And eye-opening. One thing this newer version of herself had in common with the last one was that it needed a man who had his own world sussed and wasn't afraid to stand up and be counted. As long as he didn't hurt her.

Nathan knew he'd overreacted to Molly O'Keefe's false smile about the barbecue, but he'd had enough of those. Two months and not once had she joined the staff for a meal, let alone anything else, despite everyone trying to persuade her. Whether she thought she was too good for them, or she believed she wasn't good enough, the jury was still out.

Yet she'd been quick to sign up for the barbecue. Part of him questioned whether she'd actually show up; another suggested maybe Molly didn't back down once she'd taken a stance. Despite working alongside her, often in trying circumstances, he didn't know her at all, which was unusual given the work they did. She didn't fall over backwards to get on with him. That might make him egotistical, but nothing added up. He got on well with most folk, and socialised enough not to return to being the hermit he'd become after Rosie's death.

Molly's a challenge.

He stumbled, righted himself, his eyes seeking out the woman doing this to him. Did he want her to like him? Now, *that* sounded needy. Hardly true when he had his pick of friends, even women. His gaze cruised across the department to the locker-room door from where a burst of laughter came. Vicki was doing her best to be happy on her thirtieth birthday, but her heart was sad because Cole was supposedly deployed offshore with the army.

He couldn't wait to see her face when he dropped his best friend off at their apartment this afternoon. It would be a big surprise, one he couldn't justify when he saw the sadness lurking in the back of Vicki's eyes. He'd prefer to tell her the truth, and have her meet Cole, but he'd given his friend his word, and promises were not to be broken.

Molly appeared in the doorway, a rare genuine smile lighting up her face and causing those emerald eyes to sparkle, though she'd glared at him earlier. He shouldn't have pushed her buttons but, hell, it'd been impossible not to when he was exhausted after eight hours dealing with what felt like half of Sydney coming through the ED's doors.

Molly rattled him in ways he couldn't believe. He was not used to having his libido captivated by a woman who wasn't interested in him. What libido? Since Rosie's death there'd been little going on in that department, and when there was it was for relief, not involvement. He couldn't imagine being lucky enough to find love for a second time, hadn't been ready to consider it because who got that lucky? Yet today Molly had him questioning that.

Nathan shrugged. So there might be more nous behind Nurse O'Keefe's non-confrontational looks and that beautiful, heart-stopping face than he thought. He should've wound her up weeks ago if the flaring temper in her expression was the result. Far more interesting than quiet and mousy, as he'd believed. A shiver ripped down his spine, but not because her haughty glare daunted him. Not a bit. Instead it gave him a sharp awareness of the woman behind the glare.

Molly was waking up his body, which he preferred to leave in sleep mode until *he* decided otherwise. The sense of being slightly off balance had come out of left field the day she'd started in the department, and now he'd had enough of feeling out of whack. This morning it'd been time to push her boundaries over not joining in staff events so he could get relief from these frustrating sensations. This reaction confused him, and made him feel more than annoyed. Yeah, frustrated. But as in sexually or more? He didn't have a clue.

'You all going to spend the day in there?' he called out. No way did he intend heading to the café without making sure Molly didn't do a runner, because, say what she liked, she had looked edgy for a moment. Vicki liked her a lot, so Molly doing an about-face wasn't happening.

'Pretty much. How come you waited?' Molly's enticing shoulders had returned to their normal, slightly sloped position and her chin had softened back to quiet and mousy.

Except he no longer trusted his interpretation of that look. There was more to Nurse O'Keefe than met the eye. Deep down, had he always suspected so? And reacted accordingly by keeping his barriers in place to protect himself? For better or worse, there was a need ticking inside him making it impossible to look away, or deny how she intrigued him, or pretend he did not want her in his bed, underneath him. Or on top if she preferred. Jeez. He scrubbed his hands down his face. What was wrong with him?

'You run out of words?'

Something like that. 'I'm making sure no one gets lost.'

Her smile didn't slip a notch. 'I told Vicki I'd be there, and I never go back on my word.' Then doubt—or was it guilt?—slid through her sharp gaze and she looked away.

'Glad to hear it.' What was that about? Had she let someone down? In a big way that had come back to haunt her? Behind his ribs a sense of confusion lurched and an unreal feeling of protectiveness crept over him. For Molly? Hardly. There was definitely far more to this woman than he'd realised, but why spend time wondering what made her tick when it was obvious she wouldn't have a bar of him? She was a challenge. And causing a pool of desire to settle in his gut.

Could be hunger for food doing a number on him. Not Molly. He'd missed snack breaks throughout the night—always a bad thing. But nothing was dispelling that softening sensation in his belly as he watched her. Without even trying, she was doing a number on him. Bet he was the last person she wanted to spend time with, even if only over coffee. Was it time for a change? On both their parts? Could be it was time for him to step outside his secure bubble and poke at life, see where it took him.

As long as it wasn't more than he was prepared to give. More than he was *able* to give. He'd given his heart to Rosie, and she'd taken it to the grave with her. Or so he'd believed, until—until now and the thin ray of hope beginning to pierce his long-held belief that he couldn't be that lucky.

He and Rosie had been childhood sweethearts and so in love it had been unreal at times. Except reality had got in the way of their plans for a house and babies in the form of leukaemia. From the first day Rosie had complained of lethargy and swollen, sore glands they had been on a one-way road to hell. It had been a short trip, lasting little more than three months. He'd been glad for her sake it was over quickly, but for himself he'd only wanted her never to leave him, taking his dreams away for ever.

The disease that had taken Rosie's life had a lot to answer for. He used to picture them together, raising their kids, having a great life. The past four years had been long, and lonely in a way he wouldn't have believed before she'd died.

'Nathan?'

He pulled out of his reverie to find Vicki watching him with amusement forming crinkles at the corners of her eyes. 'Yes?'

'Lead on. We're all good to go.' Her wink was slow, and downright mischievous, reminding him how she and Cole thought it was time he came out of his cave. Grabbing his elbow, Vicki strode ahead of the group, tugging him along with her.

'I'm hangry,' he warned around a smile. His friends cared about him so he let them off their interfering ways.

Vicki only laughed. 'I heard you giving Molly a bit of a roasting this morning about the winter party. One she didn't deserve, by the way.'

'Someone had to tell her to get over staying on the fringe around us.'

Vicki jabbed him with an elbow. 'Others have told you they'll be there and not signed the list. Who needs a list anyway?'

'I do.' He huffed a breath. 'Why did she do that pen-snatching thing and scrawl her name across the page large enough to suggest I might be blind?'

'To rile you? It worked, by the way.'

I know that. Damn her. 'Right.' A spurt of resentment soured his mouth. He swallowed it away, and managed to laugh at himself. So Miss Mousy had got one over him. Game on, Molly O'Keefe.

Vicki hadn't finished. 'I'm glad you nudged her about joining in. It's good for her.' Another jab from that blasted elbow. 'She needs to get out more.'

Nathan stared at his friend. 'Since when has she talked about anything that's not to do with patients?' He'd never heard Molly say something as simple as she'd been to the hair salon. And, yes, he knew when she went because those short, red curls would be quiet, in place, for a few days before returning to their riot of crazy colour. He preferred the wild to the tamed.

A tingling itch sometimes crept over his palms as he wondered about pushing his fingers through her hair. Then he'd remember he didn't have a heart any more and would go and see a patient. See? Early on she *had* disturbed him in ways only Rosie had ever done, yet they were opposites. Rosie had mostly been calm, with little that would upset her. On the other hand, Miss Quiet and Mousy, red head contrasting with her temperament and all, managed to upset his orderly existence without even trying, especially when he was overtired or pressured by a particularly ill child. As of now he was going to delete mousy from the nickname.

Vicki tapped him none too gently on the shoulder to bring his attention back to her. 'Molly lives in an apartment on the third floor of a block in Bondi Junction, takes the train to work, has a regular car that doesn't stand out at the lights, and likes to watch comedy shows on TV. Oh, and she has lots of amazing clothes that suggest a previous life that wasn't so lean.'

'You two are close.'

'Sarcasm is the lowest form of wit.' Vicki grinned. 'But you're forgiven since you're in need of food.'

Nathan shook his head. He'd learned more in two minutes than he had in the past weeks. More than Molly being a superb nurse with a special way with the younger patients that came their way so they all fell in love with her, even when she was cleaning a wound that stung or sliding a needle into their arm. He could also admit to seeing her wearing stunning—and expensive— figure-enhancing outfits when she strode onto the ward heading for the staff changing room at the beginning of her shifts. Not that her figure needed enhancing; it did a damned good job of filling out her uniform and her day clothes all by itself.

Bondi Junction, eh? And here he'd been thinking she probably lived in one of the upmarket suburbs near or on Sydney Harbour's waterfront.

Expensive clothes, average address. Once had money, now getting by? Throw in not mixing with people, the loneliness that sometimes blitzed her eyes, and he had to wonder if she'd been let down big-time. That protective instinct raised its head again. Guess he'd never know what was behind Molly's attitude since she wasn't likely to spill her guts over breakfast. Especially not to him. 'Let's hope she enjoys herself.'

'We'll do our best to make sure she does.' Another wink came his way.

'Stop that. Whatever that wicked mind of yours is coming up with, it's not happening. You have a birthday to focus on, not someone else's problems.' Suddenly Nathan was more than pleased Molly was here. He understood loneliness, knew how it could drag a person down deep. After Rosie had died he'd holed up in their home, only coming out to attend lectures or work a shift at the hospital, doing what was required to qualify—no more, no less. None of his friends or family had been able to prise him out into the real world to become involved with people and life other than what was required for patients and qualifying as an emergency specialist.

To get past the pain of losing Rosie he'd focused entirely on those things and it had worked for the first couple of years. Then he'd begun to understand he wasn't any use to the people who needed his medical skills if he didn't get out and about, and that he owed the people he loved for sticking around.

'We're having champagne this morning.' Vicki laughed.

'Already sorted,' he agreed, his mood lightening further in anticipation of spending time with this group of chatterboxes.

And Molly. No, forget that. She wouldn't start yabbering on to him. Maybe by the end of breakfast they'd be a little further ahead in knowing each other, but that was all. Bet she'd still have his hands tingling and his gut tightening, though. 'Shows we're in need of a life when this is as exciting as it gets.'

Nathan hated admitting it, but he'd been looking forward to breakfast. His heart felt lighter, and the blood seemed to move faster in his veins. Molly had nothing to do with the happy sensations in his chest, or the sudden urge to be on his best, most charming behaviour. *That* needed a bit of practice anyway, and she'd see straight through him and ignore his attempts.

CHAPTER TWO

AS THE GROUP approached the café entrance, Molly smoothed down her trousers and jacket, hauled her shoulders back so that she looked and felt confident, before following everyone inside to the reserved table where Nathan was pulling out a chair on the far side.

Why did she seek him out? Because his mood had improved? Out of doctor mode and into something friendlier, less gruff than usual. Still handsome and mouth-watering. He didn't often come across as too confident and charming, even though he could enchant a screaming patient into quietly accepting an injection and his medical knowledge was second to none. Experience had taught her to look behind a man's character traits to find out what really made him tick.

'Vicki?' Nathan indicated the chair he'd pulled out.

'The birthday girl gets to sit at the top of the table.' Hank pulled out another chair.

'You're right.' Vicki grinned and sat down on Hank's chair. 'Molly, why don't you take that chair Nathan's holding?'

Because Nathan had already slung his jacket over the one next to it. Looking around the table, Molly saw seats were filling rapidly, leaving her little choice. *Fake it...* Forcing a smile on her mouth and lifting her chin like nothing was wrong in her world—because it wasn't any more—she strolled around to plonk down on the chair Nathan was holding out. 'Thanks.'

'You want a coffee?' he asked, surprise and something else she couldn't interpret flitting across his face.

Thoughtlessly putting a hand on his arm, she said, 'I'll get it.' She jerked away. She never touched a man. Showed how safe she felt around Nathan, despite his attitude.

He said in his I'm-here-to-help-you voice usually reserved for patients, 'I'm going to check the champagne I've ordered to toast Vicki's birthday is coming out soon. I'll put our coffee orders in at the same time.' His gaze was intent, his eyes searching for something in her expression.

Okay, lighten up. 'That'd be great. A flat white, thanks.' Her tongue felt far too big for her mouth. Just another way he tipped her world off its new axis. 'Are we all putting in for the champagne?' But he was gone, slipping through the crowd building around other tables, aiming for the counter, head and shoulders above everyone he passed.

Since she'd run away from Paul she hadn't gone out with a man, never let one in her home or talked about her past to anyone. At first she'd struggled facing the world as most people she knew had blamed her for Paul's arrest. He was so charismatic they'd believed him until the truth had come out in court and those same people had begun fawning over her, wanting to get back onside. She'd struggled not to turn bitter. At the time, dating men had been an impossibility.

Until now. Looking at Nathan, she thought he'd be protective of those he loved. He always stood up for a patient whenever a family member tried to force proceedings in the department that were wrong. No doubt he'd protect anybody who got into danger if he was close by.

Downright crazy to believe that without proof. Look what happened the last time I trusted a man.

Paul hadn't been kind and gentle with those less fortunate than himself, instead he'd enjoyed showing how much better than others he was. Something she hadn't seen until it had been too late. Hadn't known to look. Paul had been the catch every woman wanted, and with her mother actively encouraging her, she'd gone for him and won. Then lost. The first year of her marriage had been bliss, then the cracks had started appearing. She was a lousy hostess, a simpleton, useless at any damned thing. Then she'd fallen pregnant and it was all over.

Molly shook her head. *Stop right now.* She was out with a bunch of great people. She needed to forget the self-pity and enjoy herself, not turn in on herself and repeat the mistake she'd made with the Roos, the basketball team she'd been a member of. The regret she felt every weekend when she looked up the team's results from the Saturday game made her ache, made her wish she'd stopped worrying about letting anyone close for fear of being hurt and got on with enjoying being a part of a great bunch of women. If only she hadn't given in and quit, she might've moved on with getting a life sooner.

So, get cracking and enjoy this morning.

Straightening her spine and breathing deeply, she then fell into another old habit, checking out the latest suits to walk into the café, swinging briefcases and checking their phones. But today she wasn't looking for trouble, instead comparing the men with Nathan. He came out top every time. Something to think about once she was back in her apartment.

'Here you go. Coffee's on the way.' A glass

of water appeared before her. 'As is the champagne,' Nathan told Vicki.

'Great.' Molly sat up straighter. Today she might even celebrate her divorce. One sip of champagne for that, and no one at the table would be any the wiser.

Her gaze returned to Nathan, and instantly her heart forgot that memo about not thumping too hard. Crazy. He was just another male she worked with—one who happened to be bone-meltingly good looking, and currently making her aware of him in ways she'd hadn't known around men for a long time. Yet there was something about him that had her wondering what it would be like to curl up against his chest, be held in those strong arms and just relax, be happy. No, it wasn't happening. She wasn't ready. Could she give it a go? Probably not.

Nathan handed her a menu. 'Here, take a look. Most of us know this off by heart. There are some great choices.'

'Suddenly I'm starving.' Molly began scanning the page.

Nathan grunted. 'I'm past hungry. Could eat a whole sirloin.'

She laughed. 'How about tofu and grains?'

His eyes widened. He hadn't thought she'd tease him? Last week she wouldn't have. 'You can't pull that one. Like I said, I've been here before.'

'Okay, so one whole sirloin, and what?' The whole steak wasn't on offer, but he could order two helpings. 'Chips or hash browns, as well as eggs and bacon?'

'Stop right there.' He was smiling directly at her, and it was making her stomach feel like hot chocolate dropped into cream, swirling, warming, tempting. 'Don't mention food like that when I'm this hungry.'

'But you're smiling.' When she was starving she couldn't smile.

'Don't trust it.'

Sorry, Nathan, but I do believe you. Gazing at him, and especially at his smile, Molly felt no qualms. No fear of him erupting into a rage because he needed to eat now, not in ten minutes. Again, she felt that rare sense of safety around him. Needing to put mental space between them, she'd join in the conversations going on around her and enjoy the birthday celebration. After she told the hovering waitress she'd like the eggs Benedict, that was.

The room was crowded, with a queue waiting at the counter for take-out coffees and pastries. In their corner her group was out of the way and could talk without yelling. The champagne arrived and glasses were filled.

Nathan stood up. 'Happy birthday, Vicki. May all your wishes come true.'

Vicki blinked. 'Thanks. I only have one, and it's not happening.' Another blink, and she raised her glass. 'Cheers, everyone, and thank you for joining me today.'

Molly wanted to hug Vicki and wipe away that sadness. Spontaneous hugs not being her thing any more, the best she could manage was to have fun, and not bring her past into the room. Suddenly she was very glad she'd come. Today she'd started to live, not just exist. It was a tiny step in the right direction, but it was a bigger step than usual. There'd be plenty more. Yes, there would.

Nathan sat down and picked up his glass of water. 'Anyone want to start singing "Happy Birthday"? Not me, I'd empty the place.'

'That'd make it a memorable day for Vicki,' someone joked.

Without a thought, Molly began singing 'Happy Birthday'. Instead of everyone joining in, they stared at her. She faltered to a stop. 'What's wrong?'

'Nothing,' everyone cried. 'Carry on.'

Embarrassed, she shook her head and sipped her water. 'Someone else can have a turn.'

'Not after that, they can't,' Nathan muttered. 'You sing like an angel.'

For a moment she forgot everything except the memories of singing, especially with Gran, and how happy it had made her. 'I inherited my grandmother's singing gene.' Gran had paid for her lessons until she'd decided she didn't want music as a career but rather a happy go-to place. 'She sang for the national opera company.' She'd also been the only one to question her love for Paul before the wedding.

Not now, Moll. Having fun, okay?

She turned to Nathan. 'That's some car you've got. I saw you arrive at work last Wednesday when I drove in for a change.'

Again he was watching her intently, but at least there was no tension lurking behind his gaze this time. *And* he went with her change of subject. 'Not bad, eh? I only bought it a month ago and haven't had time to take it for a spin out on the highway. But it has to happen soon, or else I might as well sell it.'

'That'd be a waste.' She couldn't think of anything more exciting than speeding along the road in that amazing car, forgetting everything and enjoying the moment.

Wrong, Moll. Being with Nathan would be more exciting.

Molly spluttered into her coffee.

Nathan held out a serviette. 'Here, wipe your face.'

Trying to snatch the paper serviette from his fingers only caused her to touch him, and she pulled back. Heat that had nothing to do with stopping the spluttering and everything to do with longing began unfurling deep inside her. It came with a growing awareness of herself as a woman, and of the man beside her. 'You a dad, by any chance? You have a thing about goo on faces?'

The serviette was scrunched into a ball and dropped back on the table. 'No kids,' he muttered and looked away.

Back to upsetting him. She didn't know what to say for fear of further annoying him. Time to talk to someone else. Leaning forward, she eyeballed Emma across the table. 'When do you head over to Queenstown?' The intern was going to New Zealand's winter festival.

'Thursday. I can't wait. Have you been?'

'Years ago. It's an amazing event in an extraordinary location.'

Nathan wasn't going to be ignored. 'Did you go on the jet boat?'

'Of course.'

'You're obviously into speed.' When he smiled his whole face lit up in a way she rarely saw.

'I guess I am. Not that I've done anything extreme. Nor will I be. Safe and sensible is me.'

'Nothing wrong with that.' Nathan was watching her in a way that suggested he wanted to know more about what made her tick outside work. But he waited, didn't push.

Which had her opening up a little. 'I liked my sports, sailing on large yachts, going to rock concerts, things like that.'

'Liked?' he asked quietly. 'Not any more?'

Thump. Reality check. Hurrying to deflect him, she spluttered, 'Still like, but I don't seem to find the time any more. Neither do I know anyone in Sydney with a yacht the size I'm used to.' Actually, she did, but that family was part of the past, so she wasn't paying them a visit any time soon. In fact, never.

'I don't suppose a three-metre Paper Tiger would suffice?' Nathan wasn't laughing at her, just keeping the conversation going on a comfortable level, like he was trying to stop her tripping into the black hole that was her past. He couldn't be. He knew nothing about it. 'My brother-in-law's got one.'

A laugh huffed across her lips, surprising her. 'Me? Actually sail a small yacht? I don't think so. I'd probably fall off or drop the sail at the wrong moment.'

'All part of learning to sail.' He grinned, then told her about his misadventures on his surfboard.

* * *

Nearly an hour later people had finished eating, and were beginning to gather their gear together.

'Guess it's time to head away,' Molly said reluctantly. It had been fun talking and laughing with everyone, but especially with Nathan. He was different away from work, more at ease with her somehow, talking about Queenstown, his car, and other things. He even laughed and smiled often. He was a man she liked and wanted to spend more time learning more about.

Nathan leaned closer, said quietly, 'Feel like a ride in my car?' There was a cheeky smile on that divine mouth, and something in his eyes that asked if she was up to it. 'I can drop you home.'

Molly's mouth dropped open. She snapped it closed. Then spluttered, 'That's not necessary. I'm fine with the train.'

Across the table Vicki rolled her hand from side to side. 'Train or top-of-the-range sports car. I know which I'd prefer.'

So did she. Except the car meant being squashed into a confined space with a man. Not just any man. Nathan. Standing up, she said, oh, so casually, 'It's a long way to Bondi Junction.'

'It's on my way. I live in Coogee.' When she raised her eyebrows, he continued in a voice that suggested he was determined she'd go with him,

'I didn't even finish one glass of champagne so you don't have to worry about my driving.'

'I wasn't.'

Nathan shrugged. 'Let's fix our bills and get the car.'

'Nathan, you don't have to do this.' At least he hadn't offered to pay for her meal. Thank goodness for something, because she'd have argued hotly. Paying her own way meant never owing anyone anything. Her stomach was doing a squeeze and release thing, while her head spun with the thought she'd be crammed into a car with a male she didn't know very well. With Nathan Lupton, sex on legs, kindness in his heart and, don't forget, someone who was quick to get grumpy with her, but who she trusted not to hurt her.

'You said you like fast cars.'

True. She couldn't contain the smile splitting her face. Her first car had been a racy little number bought by her mother for her eighteenth birthday. She'd loved it. 'But you can't get up any speed between here and my apartment.'

'Now, there's a challenge.' He smiled back and flipped a coin in the air, caught it and laughed.

Nathan watched the conflicting emotions zipping across Molly's face and damned if they didn't make him want to spend more time with her, not to prove he could win her over but because he just might like her. The challenge was heating up. Though not in the way he'd intended. The offer of a ride home was because on and off throughout breakfast he'd warmed to her more and more, therefore he didn't want the morning to end.

Today Molly intrigued him. He was not walking away. Nope. The genuine happiness lightening her gaze throughout breakfast had stirred him in places usually unaffected by other people, and had him wishing for more, had him remembering he'd once had a heart and thinking he just might like to get it back—if he could find the courage. She'd be a keeper, if he wanted to get involved, and that was the problem. He didn't. Here was the rub. He might be ready to start dating on a regular basis but the thought of anything permanent still freaked him out. To fall in love and have his heart torn out of his chest a second time was unimaginable.

'Ready when you are.' The smile lifting the enticing corners of Molly's soft mouth was real, and not that strained, 'smile if I absolutely have to' version she was so good at. Seemed she'd quite quickly got over trying to talk him out of giving her a lift.

Because he wanted to believe Molly's smile had been for him, he'd risk being hit over the head by teasing her. 'You could seem more excited.'

'Sure.' She leaned in to give Vicki a hug. 'Happy birthday. If you need some company later, give me a call.'

Vicki's eyes lit up. 'I might just do that. Shoe shopping comes to mind.'

Molly was looking surprised about something. It wouldn't be shoes. Everyone knew of Vicki's fetish for footwear. Something else had put the stunned look on her face.

'You could do worse than hanging out with Vicki.'

She glanced down at her high-heeled, black-with-a-bow shoes. 'I reckon.' Then she looked back at him and shrugged, said with caution in her voice, 'No time like now to get back into it.'

Get back into friendships? Again that protective need nudged, stronger this time. He felt certain something had gone amiss with Molly, something that kept her on edge and wary around her colleagues. 'Vicki, you right for getting home?'

That cheeky grin flicked from him to Molly, then disappeared, unhappiness replacing it. 'I'm fine.'

Only because his car was a two-seater, he nodded. 'See you around three.'

'You don't have to coddle me because it's

my birthday. Anyway, I'm going shopping with Molly.'

'Yes, I do.' Or Cole would have his guts for guitar strings. 'Shop as much as you like but be home when I get there.'

Molly eyed first him then Vicki, who gave her a big smile before heading out the door. 'You two are close.' Something strangely like envy darkened her voice.

'Her husband's been my best mate from years back when we were into surfing. We continued our friendship into med school, and never stopped since.' Cole had been there for him in the darkest days. Taking Molly's elbow, he kept his touch light when he longed to pull her closer and breathe in that rich fragrance that was her. Funny but he hadn't realised how often he'd smelled it until now. She really was doing a number on him, and didn't have a clue. Which was something to be grateful for. That, and not how he was spending time with her, breaking down the barrier she kept between them.

'You don't surf now?' When she tilted her head back to stare up at him it was almost impossible not to reach across to tuck some wayward curls behind her ear.

Resisting required effort, so it took time to answer. 'Occasionally I chase a wave out where I live but not as often as I used to. Cole joined the army and I broke an ankle. That didn't prevent me getting back on the board once the bones mended, but around that time specialised study began taking up all my spare hours.'

What was left had been for Rosie. Rosie. His heart wavered. The love of his life. Nothing like Molly. Would he have taken a second look if she had been? It would be too strange.

Hang on. *Second* look? There'd been a third, fourth and more. He shivered, suddenly afraid of where this might lead. All the moisture in Nathan's mouth dried up. He might be getting closer to stepping off the edge in the hope of finding that deep, loving happiness he'd once known, but what if it all went sour? Turned to dislike instead? Or worse, what if he fell in love with a woman he couldn't make happy because of his past?

They reached his car. 'What's your address in Bondi Junction?'

'I'll put it in the GPS.' Molly settled into the seat and buckled in. 'I know the way, but let's play it safe.' Seemed she wanted to get there as soon as possible.

They didn't talk on the way, but when he pulled up outside the apartment block Molly indicated, he said, 'I'll walk you to the entrance.' The sooner the better. He needed to breathe air not laden with Molly's scent, and to put space between them. Then drive away, windows lowered and music on loud. He needed to stop, think about what he was doing getting to know Molly, before it got out of hand.

'That's not necessary.' She grabbed her bag from the floor and elbowed the door open, snatching up the hairbrush that had fallen out of her bag.

The door shut with a soft click, but Nathan was already moving around to join her on the pavement. 'When I see someone home I go all the way.'

Her emerald eyes widened as something akin to laughter sparkled out at him. 'We don't know each other well enough for that.'

'You know what I meant.'

That was not disappointment blinking out at him. It couldn't be. Then Molly proved it wasn't. 'That's a relief. I wasn't a hundred percent sure what you were saying.' Her eyes cleared, but there was a little twitching going on at the corners of her mouth.

Hell, he'd love to kiss that mouth. He needed to know if those lips were as soft and inviting as they looked. His upper body leaned forward without any input from his brain, but as he began to lift his arms, common sense stepped in. Molly would kick him where no man wanted a shoe if he followed through.

Stepping back, he looked around the area. The entrance was accessed immediately off the footpath where a bus stop was outlined. Nothing wrong in that, but it was so ordinary and Molly was anything but. He sighed, long and slow. It had nothing to do with him where she chose to live. This was getting out of hand. He was making up stuff without Molly saying a word. But he had to ask, 'How long have you lived here?'

She was focused on a pebble, rolling it round on the pavement with the toe of one classy shoe, then, raising her head, she eyeballed him. 'Since I moved to Sydney a year ago. I worked in a medical centre down the road while looking for a job in an emergency department anywhere in the city.'

'I'd have thought there'd be plenty of opportunities in that time. You picky, or something?' He added a smile to take the heat out of his question.

'I got a job within weeks of starting at the medical centre, but a nurse I worked with came down with leptospirosis and when the manager asked me to stay on until she was back up to speed I didn't feel I could let them down. They'd been nothing but good to me from day one.'

How many questions could he get away with? Pushing her wasn't being fair, but he needed to learn more. Maybe the answers would dampen the ardour taking hold of him. 'I'd have thought you'd move closer to the city, where the shops and nightclubs are.'

'I like it out here.' For the first time he heard doubt in her voice. 'Neither do I mind the train trip. It doesn't take long. Judging by the traffic the few times I've driven in, I think the train probably gets me there in less time than it takes you in that fancy car.'

True. 'Where did you move from?' So much for shutting up.

'Adelaide. Before that, Perth.' The pebble flicked across the path as she turned away. 'I'm heading inside for some sleep. Thanks for bringing me home.'

His heart skittered. What was wrong with his last question? 'Wait.' What the hell for? Despite the tightening in his belly and groin brought on by those curves outlining her jacket and trousers, he had to let her go. He wasn't ready for this. He'd bet Molly wasn't either.

She paused to look over her shoulder. 'Go home, Nathan. Get some sleep too. Being Friday, tonight's bound to be hectic.'

Ignoring that, he said, 'You want to come with me sometime when I take this…' he waved at his car '…for a blast along the highway?' What happened to not ready, and thinking things through? Damned if he knew, other than he wasn't giving up that easily now that he'd started.

She stared at him as if he'd just asked her to fly to the moon in a toy box.

He waited, breath stalled between his lungs and his nostrils, hands tightening and loosening. What was the problem? He'd asked Molly to go for a spin, which meant sharing the small space and breathing her scent some more. No big deal. Yet it felt huge. It was a date. So what? *About damned time.* There'd been the occasional romp in the sack with women who understood that was all he was offering.

He knew instinctively that Molly would not want that with him. Then again, maybe she would, and he could have fun and walk away afterwards. Shock hit him in the gut. He didn't want that with this woman. All or nothing. No half-measures. *All* had to be out of the question. She wasn't his type. So it had to be nothing. About to withdraw his offer of a ride, he got a second shock.

Molly was grinning at him, and it was the most amazing sight. Beautiful became stunning, quiet became gorgeous and cheeky. 'Only if I get a turn at the wheel.'

His heart must've stopped. Nothing was going on behind his ribs. His lungs had seized. It didn't surprise him when his knees suddenly turned rubbery. How could he refuse her? Leaning back against the car to prevent landing in a heap on the damp asphalt, he asked, 'You like driving fast?' Fast and dangerous? He hadn't thought dangerous would come into anything Molly did. She appeared too cautious. Appeared, right? Not necessarily correct.

'Strictly safe and sensible, that's me.' The grin dipped.

Phew. He could get back on track, be the colleague who'd brought her home—and ignore the challenge he'd set himself. If only Molly's mouth hadn't flattened, because that got him wanting to make her smile again. 'I promise I'll be so safe you'll want to poke me with needles.' He straightened, took a tentative step and, when he didn't fall over, began walking up to the main door, making sure Molly was with him.

He got no further than the entrance.

'Thanks, again.' Molly punched a set of numbers into the keypad.

'I'll see you to your apartment.'

'I'm on the third floor. Think I can manage,' she muttered. 'See you tonight.' The lock clicked and she nudged the wide door open. 'I'm glad I went to breakfast. It was fun.'

Warmth stole across his skin and he had to refrain from reaching out to touch her. 'Glad you came. Now, I'd better get going. I've got things to do before I pick Cole up from the airport.'

A frown appeared between those fall-into-them eyes. 'I thought he wasn't going to be around for her birthday.'

'It's a surprise. He managed to wangle a weekend's leave. The rest of his contingent is on the way home via Darwin, while he's coming direct from KL.'

'There goes the shopping.' Molly smiled. 'She can't work tonight.'

'I organised that without letting slip what's going on. I'll tell her when I drop Cole off.'

'Good on you. It'd be awful if she had to waste this opportunity of having time out with her man.' Though filled with longing—for what, he had no idea—at least Molly's sigh was better than her quiet, mousy look.

Not mousy. Not any more. Sauntering towards his car, he called over his shoulder, 'See you tonight.' Time to put distance between them before he did something silly, like ask why it had taken weeks for her to front up and socialise with the people she worked with. That would put a stop to getting closer.

Nathan remained beside his car until Molly went inside and the door had closed behind her. Then he got in and drove on to Coogee and his small piece of paradise, his mind busy with all things Molly. She'd tipped him sideways by wanting little to do with him.

Except go for a spin in this beast.

No matter what else came up, he'd find time to follow through on that. Hopefully this weekend, so he could get to spend time unravelling the façade Molly showed the world.

Don't think that's going to happen in a hurry. Better remember to get her number tonight.

Pulling up at traffic lights, Nathan tapped the steering wheel in time to the rock number playing on the radio. A strident ringing from the passenger side of the car intruded. Leaning over, he fossicked around until his fingers closed over a phone. Had to be Molly's. His finger hovered over the green circle, but of course he couldn't answer it. If for no other reason than she'd kill him.

A smile slowly spread across his face. Now he had a reason to return to her apartment and speak to her, and get her phone number at the same time.

CHAPTER THREE

'HOT DAMN.'

Molly leaned back against her apartment door as it clicked shut and tried not to think about Nathan. Like that was going to happen.

A grin spread across her face. What a morning. They'd gone from grumping to talking to smiling and then he'd driven her home and insisted on walking to the entrance with her. He'd have come up here if she'd let him.

She looked around the tiny space, smaller than Gran's chicken coop, and sighed, glad he wasn't seeing this. The shoddy apartment block would've already given him reason to wonder why a nurse on a reasonable wage would choose to live here. But it was ordinary, wouldn't attract attention.

She kept the apartment simply furnished with the bare basics in an attempt to make the rooms feel larger. The polished wood furniture came from her grandmother's cottage after Gran died.

The furniture had lain in storage until Molly had moved to Adelaide and set up house on her own. The only good thing about Gran's passing was that she didn't get to hear she had been right about Paul. She would've gone after him with her sewing scissors.

No one came to the apartment. Lizzie, her best friend back in Perth, kept saying she'd visit but never managed to make it happen with her job taking her offshore for weeks at a time. Molly missed her more than anyone from her previous life. They'd done so much together, shared a lot of laughs and tears, always been there for one another. But, more important, Lizzie had believed her right from the beginning when she'd said Paul hit her, and she hated him almost as much as Molly did.

Paul Bollard. Nathan Lupton. They were nothing alike. One evil. The other caring. Both could be charming, strong, over-confident. That spooked her. Paul had wooed her as though she had been a princess, at first making her feel like one. Nathan confused her, sometimes making her cross and occasionally, especially this morning, all soft on the inside.

She huffed the air out of her lungs. Nathan wasn't wooing her and, by the expressions that crossed his face at times, had no intention of doing so. Fine. With a hideous marriage behind her, the wedding ring long gone in the bin, as of this week she was single and wanting to trust and love again, but she was very, very cautious.

Going out to breakfast had been the best thing to happen to her in a long while. She worked with a great bunch, and from now on she'd attend every get-together anyone proposed. She'd also get involved with more than the charity shop. Fake it till she made it. This latest and final version of herself would not be the socialite of the past, or the cowering abused woman. Married two years, separated for two, now alone. If nothing else, she'd become more caring and understanding of other people. Mrs Molly Bollard was gone for ever.

In the kitchenette she filled the kettle for a cup of tea. Sleep would be elusive while her mind was going over the morning. Pride lifted her chest. She'd managed to fit in with her workmates to the point she'd relaxed enough to forget everything that had brought her to that point. So much so, she'd even managed to sing 'Happy Birthday'. Now, there was a step in the right direction, and she mustn't stop at that. There was a city out there to get to know, and if she was careful not to keep her distrust to the fore, she didn't have to carry on being alone, could make friends in all facets of her life.

Did Nathan go to the meals every time the

staff got together? She chuckled. He wouldn't do the shopping expeditions. She mightn't be fully ready for a partner or even a lover, but spending time over a meal with a man who laughed, grumped, looked out for others, could not be time wasted.

The doorbell chimed. Molly spun around. No one visited her. Bang went her heart. Crunch went her stomach.

Knock, knock. 'Molly, it's Nathan. I've got your phone.'

Relief prodded her towards the door. How had he managed to get inside and up to her floor without knowing the apartment number? Peering through the peephole, she got a grainy view of the man who'd driven her home.

'Molly?' That familiar irritation was back.

She opened the door. 'Sorry to be a pain. It must've fallen out of my bag with my hairbrush.'

Nathan was watching her with that intensity that was more familiar than his smiles. 'You had a call. That's how I found it.'

'A call?' she asked. 'Who from?'

He shrugged. 'I didn't look. Figured you'd be cross if I did.'

'You bet,' Molly admitted sheepishly as she checked out the caller ID. An unknown number. Her smile snapped off.

'Problem?'

'What?' She shook her head and glanced up at Nathan to soak up the warmth in his gaze. 'No. Wrong number probably.' As far as she knew, Paul only had access to the prison phone and that number was definitely in her contacts file so she could ignore it if he tried to get in touch. Anyway, he'd stopped calling her after his guilty verdict. Though who knew what receiving the divorce notice might've done to his narcissistic brain. He hated losing control over her more than anything.

The kettle whistled. Molly glanced toward the kitchenette. 'Thanks for this.'

Nathan stepped through the door. 'You into minimalist?'

Closing her eyes, she counted to four. Nathan should have left, not come inside. Yet it didn't feel wrong. More like it was okay for this man to be inside her home; as if she wanted him here. Which was so far out of left field she had to stop and look at him again. All she saw was the good-looking man who'd brought her home gazing around her apartment as if it was a normal thing to do. It probably was, for most people. That had to be in his favour. She was not thinking about the pool of heat in her stomach. Not, not, not. 'I'm making tea. Do you want one?' Ah, okay, maybe that heat was getting the upper hand.

He hesitated, his gaze still cruising her living room.

He was going to say no. She got in first. 'It's okay. You've got things to do before picking up Cole.' She wanted to feel relieved, but it was disappointment settling over her.

'Thought you'd never ask.' His gaze had landed back on her. His hands were in his pockets, his stance relaxed, yet there was something uncertain about him, like he didn't know if he was welcome. Nothing to make her afraid, more the opposite. If such a strong, confident man could feel unsure then he was more real, human—flawed in a good way. 'White with one.'

Her disappointment was gone in a flash. Replaced by a sudden longing for another chance at love. Truly? Yes, truly. Still had to go slowly, though. Turning her back on him before she fell completely under his spell and screwed up bigtime, she said, 'Would you mind shutting the door? I don't like leaving it open. Never know who might wander in.'

'No problem.' A moment later, 'In case you're wondering, it was the old lady three doors down who told me which door to knock on after I described you.'

'I guess that goes with the territory.' She'd have to talk to Mrs Porter about telling strangers which apartment was hers. Except Nathan stood in the middle of her tiny one-bed home, waiting for a mug of tea. Not a stranger. 'Take a pew.' She nodded at the pair of wooden chairs at her tiny, gleaming wooden dining table. Her mouth dried as he sat and stretched those endless legs half across the kitchenette.

'Not a lot of space for a party, is there?' He smiled.

She could get to like those smiles far too much. They warmed her in places that had been cold for a long time, places she'd held in lockdown for fear of making another hideous mistake. Reaching for the two mugs on the tiny shelf above the bench, she answered, 'As partying wasn't on my agenda when I needed a roof over my head, I'm not complaining. This suits me fine in that respect.'

He looked around again. 'You're not happy with your neighbour telling people where you live.'

'I'm a bit circumspect about giving out personal info to any old body.' Shut up. Too much information. She was not telling Nathan why she felt that way. Anyway, she needed to move on from all that. Paul was locked up. No one else wanted to hurt her.

Nathan was watching her, apparently casually, yet she'd swear he wasn't missing a thing going on in her head. 'I suppose you wouldn't want just anyone turning up unannounced.'

She needed to be on guard around him. Always. 'Exactly.' Glancing around the room that had gone from tiny to minuscule the moment he'd entered, a flicker of yearning rose. Everything about her lifestyle since moving to Sydney had been average. Average suburb, average apartment, average car. Her job was a lot better than that, but the one at the medical centre had been on a par with the other things in her life. Nobody noticed average, which had been the intention. Except now she was restless.

'I like it here, but it might be time to move somewhere more spacious, a place I can feel more connected. I come and go every day, along with everyone else in the apartment block, and all we ever do is nod and smile at each other.' Once, that had been perfect. Now it seemed to roll out in front of her like an endless dark mat leading to a door going nowhere.

'Where would you like to live?'

The phone rang, saving her from having to find an answer. The idea was new, and using Nathan as a sounding board would be stretching their new relationship a bit far. But then, this morning she'd have laughed if anyone had told her he'd be sitting in her apartment drinking tea right now.

There was no caller ID on her phone, only the same unknown number as previously. It wouldn't be anything untoward, would it? 'Hello?' Molly said, hearing the caution in her voice and forcing a smile on her face. 'Molly O'Keefe speaking.' Easier to be brave when Nathan was sitting opposite her.

'Hi, Molly. It's Jean from the charity shop. The shop phone's playing up so I'm using my personal one.'

Relief threaded through the tension that had begun tightening her body. 'What can I do for you?'

'You said to call if we got stuck for staff. One of the ladies who works Mondays has been called away to look after her sick mother. Is it possible you could help out?'

'I'd love to. I have to be at the ED by three. Does that work for you?'

'Perfect. Thank you so much. See you then.' A dial tone replaced Jean's voice. Just like that?

She dropped the phone on the table. 'That takes care of Monday morning.'

Nathan was looking at her as though expecting more from her.

'I put in a few hours at a charity shop that supports the women's refuge. Fill shelves, run up sales. That sort of thing.' The shop raised quite a lot of money for abused women and their kids, and it gave Molly a sense of satisfaction to contribute to people she understood all too well without having to explain herself. Though sometimes she suspected Jean had figured out why she turned up.

'Go, you,' Nathan said. Then a frown appeared. 'You must get to hear some horror stories. I don't think I could cope with those.'

She hesitated, torn between dodging the bullet and being honest. 'Most of the people I meet come in to spend money and support the charity. Rarely are they the women who've survived abuse. Those who have don't usually talk about it.' *Stop*. This man wasn't stupid. He'd see behind her words if she wasn't careful.

'You're probably right. The rare exceptions being those brave women who go public about their ordeals in order to raise awareness.' Awe shaded his voice, his face and that steady gaze. 'I don't know how they do it.'

'Neither do I,' she muttered truthfully.

Draining his mug, Nathan stood up. 'I'd better get cracking, get things done before heading to the airport. Sleep being one of them. You look like you're in need of some too.'

She might look tired and messy, but for once she felt more alive and awake than a toddler after a nap. Ready for fun, not sleep. Was Nathan responsible for that? Away from work she didn't get so wound up around him, took his comments on the chin. 'I might go for a run first. That always helps clear my mind.' *Anything to shake you out of my head.*

'Running doesn't wake you up?'

'Not often. I'm usually exhausted and a hot shower finishes me off.'

His eyes widened briefly. 'Right,' was all he said, but he managed one of those devastating smiles.

When she could breathe properly, she growled, 'I thought you were leaving?'

'Can't a guy change his mind?'

The smile was still going on and now her legs were starting to protest about keeping her upright. Legs that were supposed to take her for a run. The couch was looking mighty good right about now. With or without Nathan? She wanted *Nathan*? Hell, when she finally woke up she didn't do it in half-measures. There hadn't been any sex in her life for a long time and now every last cell in her body was sitting up, fighting to be noticed.

'No,' she muttered around the need clogging her throat. Not sure if the 'no' had been directed at Nathan or herself. This was not going anywhere. They worked together. He was confident, she wasn't. That was a work in progress. He'd have a woman in his life. What gorgeous-looking man didn't? She'd get over this lust as soon as he left. Or in the next hour while she was out jogging. Or while she was in bed sleeping. Or on the train going into work tonight. She would. It was only an aberration in her carefully controlled world. A damned distracting aberration, but it would pass. No choice.

'Can I have your phone number?' Nathan pulled his phone from his pocket.

So much for passing. He'd raised the ante. 'Why?'

His dark eyebrows rose. 'So I can call when I'm going to take the car for that spin. Is that all right?'

If she was supposed to be getting over her reaction to him, then why was the thought of going for a ride with Nathan winding her belly tighter than ever? Rattling off the number, she hoped she'd got it right. She could've given him the number for the zoo for all she knew. 'I'll look forward to it.' She headed for the door and hauled it open, needing to get him out of her small space where he took up all the air and made her feel tiny and fragile, and so, so alive.

Guess this was what getting a life meant. She had to pause, evaluate what was happening, figure out why she felt like this with Nathan when no one else brought on these feelings. No, no more pausing, hanging around waiting to see what the universe threw at her next. Try taking control instead. Slowly.

Nathan stepped past her, leaving a faint trail of outdoorsy aftershave scent behind him.

She gulped. Were need, desire, hope rising because she truly was attracted to him? Or was this all about getting a new life and he was merely a stepping stone? It was something else to figure out.

'See you tonight.' Quickly closing the door, she leaned against it and tipped her head back to stare at the ceiling as though the answers to her questions were written there. The excitement tripping through her veins, warming her long-frozen heart, was real. There'd been nothing slow about this debilitating sensation rocking her. Oh, no. Wham, bam, Nathan Lupton had stormed in and turned up the thermostat, taking her by surprise, and she didn't want to back off. Even if she should.

'Hell and damnation.' Nathan shook his head as he pulled into the drive and parked at the back of his large, sprawling house. Towards the end of last night's shift, quiet Molly had shown another side to herself, had become interesting. Except, having spent time with her dressed in a figure defining, classy blouse and trousers, sexy kept coming to mind, raising more questions than answers about what made her tick than anything had during the previous two months they'd worked together. From now on her stereotype uniform was not going to negate those images.

And the short time he'd spent in her apartment had him wanting to know more about where she came from, the life she'd led before moving to Sydney.

Hah. Know more? Or feel more? Touch more? Enjoy more? Learning all about her had become important. He had no idea why, except his hormones got wound up whenever she was near. Hot, alluring, *tempting* came to mind.

Temptation? The groan that spilled out of his mouth tasted of shock and disbelief. Sure, Molly was beautiful, had his hormones in a dither, but tempting? Yes, damn it all to hell and back. Because this was starting to feel like he was seriously back in the real world, where dating might happen. He'd thought for a while he might be ready, but reality was scary.

Slamming the car door harder than necessary, he strode around the house and out to the fence lining the front lawn to stare across the public green space on the other side of a wide walking path to the Tasman Sea beyond. The light breeze meant no windsurfers doing their number on the waves. Which was a shame because right now he couldn't think of anything he'd rather do than get up on a board—and no doubt fall off just as quickly, since it had been a while since he'd last surfed. At least that would occupy his mind and put these damned fool ideas to bed.

Bed? Nathan groaned. He was exhausted, and needed sleep more than anything before signing on again that night. More than thinking about Molly.

But the idea of sprawling over his couch in front of the television and trying to doze off turned his blood to thick soup. There'd be no sleep while she rampaged through his mind. The hell of it was he didn't know why she was doing this to him when up until today he'd been more likely to get annoyed with her and wish she'd pester someone else. Sure, he was annoyed with her right now, but for all the wrong reasons. So much for getting her to put that cold shoulder to rest. Instead she'd been winding him up tighter than ever. At least she didn't have a clue how badly she was rattling his cage.

You sure about that?

Good question. He'd been determined not to let her see his reactions to her, to the scent of limes from her fruit basket, to relaxing and laughing in her company.

Yeah, and what was that doubt in her face when she'd picked up her phone and seen no ID displayed? Because something *had* darkened her eyes and tightened her face. Certainly more reaction than called for by someone wanting to ask why she hadn't paid the power bill or had she forgotten she was meant to be at the dentist. One thing he knew for certain—she'd never tell him.

The apartment had been a shock. 'Poky' had the place sounding larger than it was. It was tastefully decorated, though. Was that Molly's taste? Or had she rented the place fully furnished? The late morning sun had shone through the large, sparkling windows to brighten the atmosphere. The place was spotless, her few possessions gleamed. The two mugs on the shelf, the two glasses and dinner plates, said lonely.

Turning back towards his house, Nathan hesitated. Molly had mentioned maybe looking for somewhere else to live with more space, a place that was connected to the outside world. There was a twist to her story. Maybe she came from a tight community and was missing that easy friendship with all the neighbours, except she didn't like the way the old woman had told him which apartment was hers. He looked left, right and back to his house. He knew his neighbours. While they didn't live in each other's pockets, they were there for each other if the need arose.

Don't even think it.

This place was further from work than her

apartment, which meant a bus or car to the train station.

He strode towards the back, stopped and studied his house. Slowly that familiar sense of belonging, of having found his new place in the world right here, rose, pushing other annoying emotions aside. With each front room opening out onto the veranda that ran the full width of the house with an overhanging roof, it was a haven in summer and winter.

He'd said, 'I'm buying it,' the moment the real estate salesman had pulled up outside. An impulsive purchase, made two years after Rosie's death, yet nothing had caused him to regret his decision. At the time he'd been stuck in the past, so he'd gone looking for a new home that didn't echo with Rosie's laughter.

Coogee might be a little way out of the city for travelling to work, but the vista at the end of his lawn cancelled out any annoyance about that. He'd weathered storms that had wrecked the cliffs, baked in unrelenting sun, and surfed the waves, and had finally known a quiet within himself that had been missing for far too long. The large house and sprawling, uncontained grounds were his sanctuary.

It couldn't be more different from the small, cosy, modern home he and Rosie had shared. That one had been like her; everything had had its place and the colour schemes had been perfect, the neat gardens with their carefully spaced plants drawing passers-by to lean over the fence in admiration. While this place—it was more like him. Out of sync.

No. Molly doesn't need something like this.

He didn't need Molly in his space. It wouldn't remain a tranquil place to go when the world got on top of him if temptation came to live in the attached flat.

Occasionally he had tenants for short periods, usually medical personnel moving to Sydney General from out of town who needed temporary accommodation while they got somewhere more permanent sorted. He liked it when people moved in, and he was equally happy when they left again. Easy come, easy go. It was a waste having the flat going empty, and occasionally he'd thought of asking around work to see if anyone wanted to rent it permanently, but then he'd got cold feet. What if they didn't get on? Or if the noise level increased? Or if he plain wanted his whole house to himself?

The flat's more spacious than Molly's apartment.

Molly wouldn't be noisy or intrusive. They did argue quite often. But today he'd learned they could get along just fine.

But he'd find it very difficult to ask her to

leave if the day came where he wanted to be alone.

Far safer for him to leave things as they stood.

CHAPTER FOUR

'YOU ALL RIGHT?' Nathan asked from the other side of the counter in the department's central hub where Molly was *supposed* to be writing up patient notes. Her head was so messed up with this new awareness of Nathan and wondering what he was doing that she hadn't seen him approaching.

'Couldn't be better,' she lied. 'I managed some sleep after my run.' It was true, though her kip had been filled with dreams of being held in Nathan's arms while she drove his car. Why were dreams so ridiculous? On all counts? 'What about you?'

He grimaced. 'I managed an hour before going to the airport, and then a couple more after an early dinner.'

That explained the shadows beneath his eyes. 'It goes with the territory.' Night shifts played havoc with sleep patterns.

'At least next week I'm on three to eleven.

Back to…' he flicked his fingers in the air '…normal.'

'Me, too.' She glanced at the clipboard in his hand. 'You seeing Colin Montgomery next?'

His thick, brown-blond hair tumbled over his forehead as he nodded. 'I see he's got history of arrhythmia and is presenting with palpitations and chest pain.'

Molly followed him to their seventy-one-year-old patient and immediately noted down Colin's pulse and other obs. 'Did anyone come with you to the hospital?'

Colin shook his head. 'I've lived alone since my wife died two years ago.'

'I'm sorry to hear that. What about other family?' There was nothing in the notes about relatives to contact.

He blinked, and his mouth drooped. 'My son and I haven't spoken in years. Last I heard he lives somewhere in Brisbane.'

'How long have you had arrhythmia?' Nathan read the heart-monitor printout and asked pertinent questions.

'Twelve months, give or take.'

'When did the pain start?'

'Around eleven. When it didn't ease off I phoned for an ambulance. I hope I'm not wasting everyone's time. It's very busy in here.'

'A typical Friday night,' Molly assured him.

'Never think you're wasting our time. With your known condition, it's always best we check you out.' Nathan listened to his chest through a stethoscope. 'You're on warfarin. How steady are your test results?'

'Usually my bleeding times stay within the allowable range. Prothrombin, isn't it?' He didn't wait for an answer. 'But last week the test ran really high and I had to have the test every day until the results returned to normal.'

'Although that's not normal for people not on the drug, it is within the required range for someone taking the anticoagulant drug,' Nathan explained.

Colin looked worried. 'Isn't that dangerous?'

'It's what's preventing you having a stroke. That must've been explained when you first started taking it.'

Colin looked sheepish. 'It probably was, but at the time I was too worried about everything, and not being medically minded just accepted that I needed to take the warfarin to stay alive. I could've gone on the internet to find out more but I'd have confused myself further.'

'Relax. You're not the first to react that way, and you won't be the last.' Nathan locked a steady gaze on his patient. 'I'm referring you to Cardiology so they can run more tests to find out what's going on with this pain and that spike in your prothrombin results.'

'Better safe than sorry?' Colin enquired, his worry-filled eyes glued on his doctor.

Nathan calmed him with his straightforward manner. 'I don't believe there's a major problem but I'd prefer you spent at least the rest of tonight in the hospital, where you can be monitored and not at home alone, worrying about what might or might not be going on inside your chest.' He was good. 'That'd only raise your blood pressure, which we don't want happening.'

Colin relaxed more with every sentence.

While Nathan called Cardiology, Molly went to check on eight-year-old Ollie Brown, who'd fallen out of his bunk and broken an arm. 'Hey, young man, how's that head?' There was concern he'd got a concussion as well and a scan had been ordered.

'Hurts like stink.' Ollie grinned.

The grin vanished as his grandfather snapped, 'You're not on the farm now, lad.'

Molly chuckled. 'So you're a country guy? What are you doing in the middle of Sydney, then?' She wanted to observe Ollie for signs of confusion or amnesia.

'It's the school holidays,' Ollie said, as though she was the dumbest woman out. 'Granddad always lets us come to stay so we can do townie things, like go on the ferries and eat take-out food and stuff.' There was nothing wrong with his coherence.

'You forgot to mention that fighting with your brother was why you fell out of the blasted bunk in the first place.' The granddad scowled, but there was a load of love in his rheumy eyes.

'Connor started it.'

'You know better than to let him rile you, lad.'

Molly clapped her hands. 'Okay, guys, the orderly is on his way down to take you for the scan, Ollie. Mr Brown, you can go with him, if you'd like.'

Mr Brown nodded. 'Someone's got to keep an eye on the young pup.'

Before Ollie could say anything, Molly cut in, 'I'll be here when you get back. Then the doctor will decide if you can leave.'

Suddenly the bright, brave eight-year-old slumped and looked at his grandfather. 'I don't want to stay here. I want to go home.'

'Aw, shucks, lad. You'll have a grand time. The nurses will spoil you rotten.'

Leaving them to it, Molly headed for Kath Burgess's cubicle, only to have Hazel, the only female doctor on duty, call from the hub, 'Molly, I want you with me when I examine Kath. She's spent time with you already, and I think it's important not to bring in too many new faces since you managed to calm her down.'

'I agree.' The woman had been distraught when she'd arrived, clutching her stomach like it was going to split open, howling that she might be losing her baby. It had taken ages to quieten her enough to get some obs done.

'We all heard the commotion and our first instinct was to crowd in to see what we could do, until it quickly became obvious that the screeching was lowering to sobs and you had the situation under control. Nathan and I decided not to interfere unless you called for help. We didn't want to fire her up again.' Hazel was reading the triage notes.

'Thank goodness you did. She refuses to be seen by a male doctor.' That'd immediately put Molly on notice, wondering if Kath had been abused by a man, but when she'd tried to find out she had been told she'd fallen down the stairs at the back of her house. Molly had gone straight to Hazel to explain her concerns, but as Hazel had been about to suture a deep wound in a young male's thigh, she'd flagged Kath's notes instead and kept an eye out for whoever might be going into the cubicle.

'That doesn't sound good,' Hazel commented as she led the way into the small space where

Kath lay curled up on the bed, a bunch of tissues clasped in her hand.

Closing the curtains, Molly watched Kath closely as Hazel asked questions about what had brought her to hospital.

'I fell down the steps.'

'You're complaining of abdominal pain. How did that happen?'

'There was a toolbox there, all right?' Kath's voice was rising. 'I must've landed on that.'

'You don't know for sure?'

'I did.' Tears streamed down the woman's face.

Molly's heart went out to her. If only she could hug her and say, 'Tell us everything, and we'll get you help'—but she knew where that'd lead. The police would have to be informed, and social services would send someone to help. Kath had to be ready for what that involved. It wasn't as easy as someone who hadn't been abused would believe. Of course, Molly could be wrong, but she doubted it. It was like looking into her own eyes from the past.

When Molly had removed the sheet covering Kath and lowered her jeans and panties, she stepped aside for Hazel's examination, talking softly to Kath about anything that didn't broach the subject of her husband.

Finally Hazel straightened and pulled up

Kath's clothes. 'You're not miscarrying. But I want you to remain in bed for the next few days, at least until the pain subsides. There's still a risk of miscarriage.'

'He won't be happy,' their patient said in a dead voice.

'About you staying in bed, or about not losing the baby?' Molly asked softly.

'What do you think?'

Both, if she was on the right page. But she kept quiet. Kath was getting wound up again. Better to keep her calm and only mention help was available if she was receptive.

Molly opened the curtains so they could keep an eye on her from the hub.

'Hey, you can't come in here without permission,' Hank said loudly from the other end of the department.

'Try and stop me,' came the angry voice of an unknown male.

'Come here,' Hank demanded.

'Where is she?'

Kath gasped, 'No,' and curled in on herself.

Molly asked, 'Someone you know?'

'My man. He's been drinking since early afternoon.'

Great. Just what they needed. The sound of curtains being jerked open and sliding doors rammed back made her skin crawl. He was getting closer, and it wouldn't be long before he found who he was looking for.

'Stop right there,' Hank ordered.

'This is going to be fun,' Hazel muttered.

'Stop. You are disturbing our patients.' Nathan stood at the central counter, hands tense at his sides, his feet planted slightly apart. 'Tell me who you've come to see and I'll check if you can visit.'

'You've got my wife hiding in here. I'm going to find her. Now,' the man shouted.

Kath buried her head under the pillow.

Then her husband stormed into the cubicle, the rage in his face terrifying. 'Get out of my way,' he yelled at Hazel, raising a fist.

It was instinctive. Molly saw movement out of the corner of her eye. One step closed the gap. Her arm came up, locked with the assailant's. Using his forward motion she hauled him toward her, dropped her weight forward and swung her upper body around, taking him with her, dropping him to the floor before landing on top of him, her knees pressing into his shoulders, her hand still tight around his lower arm.

Silence fell over the department.

Then the man began swearing. He struggled beneath her, trying to push her off, getting madder by the second.

She was about to be tossed aside by a raging

man who had no brakes on his temper. Then Nathan planted a foot firmly in the small of the man's back. 'Stay still.' Under his breath he added, 'Or, hell, you're going to regret it.'

She was probably the only person to hear that. Certainly the man underneath her either hadn't or didn't believe Nathan because he was still trying to get up.

Then Hank grabbed the man's flailing arms and slammed them down on the floor. 'Shut up, buster.'

Nathan tapped her lightly. 'You can get off now. We've got him.'

She did, fast, not taking her eyes off her opponent until she'd stepped away. 'Has someone called Security?' Where had they been when this guy had got into the department? Taking a break? At least one security guard had to remain at the main entrance at all times.

'Right here.' Two uniformed men raced towards them and took over.

'You okay?' Nathan asked, his hand on her elbow.

'Sure.' She nodded.

'Molly, he was going to hit me.' Hazel nudged Nathan aside to throw her arms around her and hold tight. 'I froze when I saw his arm come up.'

Molly squeezed back, a trembling starting up

in her belly and spreading throughout her body. 'Glad *I* didn't.'

Hazel stepped back and wiped her eyes. 'Seriously, you saved me. He was aiming for my face.'

'You reacted so fast, it had to be instinctive. I'm impressed.' There was something akin to awe in Nathan's voice as his hand moved from her elbow to her shoulder. 'Come and sit down. You look like you've been hit by a bus.'

Now that the adrenaline was ebbing, that was exactly how she felt. Flattened. Shocked. 'I can't believe I did that.'

'How'd you know what to do?' Nathan asked after he had her seated and parked his butt on the counter. 'One second that man was attacking Hazel and the next you threw him on the floor and sat on him.'

'Not quite. I had my knees on his shoulders.' She gulped. That had been so close. Not once had she thought about what she was doing. When she'd caught sight of that swinging arm out of the corner of her eye the rest had followed naturally. As she'd been taught to do in her judo classes. If only she'd done martial arts when she'd been with Paul, she might have stopped him in his tracks permanently. 'I saw a movement and instantly went into defence mode. I've got an orange belt in judo,' she added when she saw the confusion enter Nathan's eyes.

'That explains it.' Maybe, but that confusion remained.

Molly hastened to divert him. 'I've always wondered how I'd react if I needed to. Now I know.'

'Why did you learn judo?' Straight to the point.

'Nathan, not now. I need to get back to Kath. The attack proved what I suspected—she's being abused. She'll need reassuring her husband's not going to get near her while she's in here. We'll also have to convince her to stay in hospital for the rest of the night.'

You're talking too much. He's going to see right through you.

Molly clamped her mouth shut and tried to stand up to pull away from those warm fingers still on her shoulder, but Nathan only tightened his hold.

'Sit down. You're as pale as the walls, and shaking like a leaf in a breeze. I'm getting you a strong coffee.'

Actually, she was damned pleased with herself. Who'd have believed she could take a man down? She opened her mouth to argue, but nothing came out when she locked her eyes with Nathan's and found compassion there, and something else. Something hinting at him beginning to understand what made her tick. Her bout of verbal diarrhoea might bring unwelcome questions.

Then a shudder ripped through her. Sinking deeper onto the chair, she looked away, fidgeting with the hem of her top as nausea crept up her throat. That had been too close. What if he'd hit Hazel? Or her? The guy had been off the scale with rage. Not cold and calculating but hot and loose. Was that how he treated Kath all the time?

Molly's heart pounded. She was safe, but Kath wasn't. Seeing that man come charging through the department as though he had the right to do as he pleased with his wife had turned her blood to ice. And brought back memories of a fist hitting her stomach, slamming against her ribs, under her chin.

Nathan was crouched in front of her, his hands now covering hers. 'Your reaction's normal.'

She nodded, afraid that if she opened her mouth she'd never shut up.

'There's more to this, isn't there?'

Another nod, sharp and uncontrollable.

'Hank,' Nathan called over his shoulder. 'Molly and Hazel could do with coffee, please. Make them sweet.'

'Onto it.'

Molly glanced around, away from those all-seeing eyes in front of her. 'Hazel?'

'I'm right here, and, like you, I've got the shakes. I'm also angry and would love a chance to tell that creep what I think of him, coming in here and trying to hurt people who want to help his wife.' Hazel pulled a chair near to Molly's. 'How're you doing?'

'I'm good.' She wanted to laugh and rejoice in being strong. She wanted to cry and hide, and go home. She wanted to bury her head against Nathan's broad shoulder, breathe him in, and feel those warm muscles under his top against her face. She wanted to be comforted by this man she knew without a doubt would never hurt her. But it wasn't happening.

One, they were in the hub of the ED, surrounded by staff and patients, and there was work to do. Two, what she wanted and what she'd get might be two different things, and right now she couldn't handle the disappointment if she'd misinterpreted that look in Nathan's eyes and he put her aside. So she'd toughen up, drink her coffee and get back to work. It was the only way to go. Once the shaking stopped, and some sense of equilibrium returned to her brain. 'I'll be right in a minute.'

Nathan said, 'Don't rush. We've got you both covered until you're ready. Even if it takes the rest of the shift.' He might be talking to them both but it was her hands he was gently squeezing.

Her bottom lip trembled. 'Thanks.'

'Take pride in what you did.' His return smile slowed her stewing stomach. 'I'd rather have you on my side than against me.'

'Then you're glad we're getting on?' No trembling in her smile now. Pride was appearing. She'd been strong, had helped Hazel. Did this mean that no man would ever again hit her? Not without a fight, anyway. Her chin lifted, and she eyeballed Nathan. 'Seems things are looking up for me.' Her new life was well and truly under way.

'Here, coffee for two.' Hank placed two mugs on the counter. 'I pinched some chocolate biscuits out of the fridge as well. Thought they might be better than sugar in your drinks.'

Nathan stood up. 'I'd better see to some patients. Don't rush, either of you.'

Molly reached for her mug, paused. 'Can I suggest only female staff work with Kath? She was leery of Hazel examining her. She's not going to like any male staff approaching her.'

Nathan nodded. 'I'll ask Myra to take over.' Myra had taken Vicki's place for the night and was a midwife and nurse who did extra shifts in ED for the money.

As Nathan passed Molly to pick up a file, his hand brushed her upper arm, and when she looked at him he gave her another soft, heart-melting smile, but sorrow darkened his eyes.

Damn it, he knew. Without being told, he'd put the pieces together and come up with the correct picture. He would want to know more. Would demand to be told everything. No, he wouldn't. They worked together, they weren't best buddies or in a relationship. He might like to know but he wasn't going to ask her for details. He was a gentleman. Wasn't he? Guess she'd find out soon enough.

For the remainder of the shift Nathan had trouble remaining calm whenever he glanced around to check on Molly. Anger at an unknown man boiled up. Given half the chance he'd like to tear out of the department to go and find him, beat him to a pulp. Not that he'd ever hit anyone before, but sweet, gorgeous Molly did so not deserve to be beaten. Not that she'd said anything to suggest it'd happened, but he knew. The sudden grief that had filled her eyes as the shock of what she'd done to Kath's husband had worn off told him there was a story behind her usually withdrawn manner.

'Glad that's over.' The woman in his head

handed a file to one of the incoming shift nurses. 'I'm ready for my bed.'

Not so fast. 'I'll give you a lift home.' Nathan put on his no-nonsense voice in the hope she'd agree without an argument.

'The train will be quicker.'

He should have known it wouldn't work. 'Throw in breakfast and you'll be able to justify going the slow way.' He'd just asked her out? It might only be breakfast, but in a roundabout way it was a date. He hadn't thought before putting his mouth into gear.

So you want to withdraw the invitation?

Nathan's chest rose. No, he damned well didn't. This wasn't only about what'd happened earlier and the revelations that had come with it. He couldn't deny the need to get to know Molly better, to learn exactly who was behind that façade she presented to the world most of the time. He sucked a breath. Which only showed how deep the mire he was floundering in had become. It had happened so fast he couldn't keep up.

Molly was blinking at him like a possum caught in headlights. 'Do you mean that?'

'About breakfast? Yes. Why wouldn't I?'

'Because you're kind and probably want to be a caring boss, making sure I'm all right. If that's the case then believe me when I say I'm fine, and there's food in my fridge that'll suffice for breakfast.'

That scratched at his calm. He was not playing the boss here. He'd stepped beyond that comfortable zone—into what, he wasn't quite sure, but knew he needed to find out. 'Bet you haven't got eggs and hollandaise sauce.'

'Low blow.' There was a wariness creeping into her eyes. She was worried what he'd ask about the martial arts.

He couldn't deny he was ready to explode over what he perceived had happened in her past, but if she didn't want to talk about it, that was her prerogative and he'd accept that. 'That's me. When I want something I'll try everything in my power to get it.' *Except use my fists.*

Molly obviously had no worries on that score because she gave him an exhausted smile. 'I'd love a ride, and breakfast.'

'Why didn't you just say so?' He grinned and took her elbow, wishing he could put an arm around her shoulders and tuck her in close. But they were still in the department and already there were a couple of raised eyebrows and knowing smiles going on. Neither were they *that* close.

'Don't like to be too obvious,' Molly retorted. Then yawned. 'Thank goodness for weekends. I'm over this week.'

'Evening shift next week, here we come.' After two days off, and hopefully a ride in his car. The Blue Mountains were looking good, and the weather was forecast to be fine and crisp. 'You been to the Blue Mountains?'

'That's a long way to go for breakfast.' Her tempting mouth gave him another smile that struck under his ribs and made his heart lift its pace.

The mountains wouldn't be too far for the morning meal if they went there the day before and stayed over in a hillside lodge, enjoying the views and a superb meal, making the most of a large, soft bed throughout the night. But that wasn't happening. *Not yet.* Nathan tripped over his own flat feet. Where the hell had that come from?

You were going to get her onside, not so close you'd get to know her so well.

He hadn't forgotten, but the rules had changed the moment she'd taken Burgess down. He had yet to figure out where he went with this now. Molly was an enigma that he was getting more than interested in. First he had to find out if he was right about her past or way off the mark. It certainly explained her edginess over mixing socially with people. Until yesterday, when she'd participated in Vicki's celebration, when she'd come out of her shell in a hurry, even singing

'Happy Birthday' in front of everyone. Not that Molly had realised what she was doing at first.

Nathan followed her to the lift, and when the door closed, he tapped the button for the basement and the car park. 'You know people will talk about what happened?'

'Fingers crossed, come Monday something else will have happened that'll take everyone's attention.' She leaned against the wall, looking so tired he wanted to wrap her up and take her home for a few uninterrupted hours' sleep. Followed by…

'How about we go to Coogee for that breakfast?'

Her eyes widened. 'That's a fair way past my apartment.'

'So it is.' What would Rosie have thought of Molly? Would she have liked her? Yes, he thought, she would. Rosie had insisted he had to move on when she'd gone, wasn't to sit around feeling sorry for himself. She'd gone as far as saying bluntly, 'Find another woman to love, have that family you've always wanted. Don't live in regret for what we've lost. That would make our time together worthless.'

But should he really take Molly to his home, show her the vacant flat? Should he start thinking ahead, instead of always looking over his shoulder at the past?

CHAPTER FIVE

WHY GO TO Coogee when there were plenty of cafés near the hospital? Or in Bondi Junction. Molly watched Nathan's firm hands with their easy movements as he drove through the morning rush hour traffic. Hands that she now knew could be gentle. Shuffling further down into the luxurious leather seat, she stifled a yawn. Which was rude when Nathan was taking her out, but the night had caught up with her.

'Have you always lived in Coogee?' she asked, in need of a distraction to stay awake. Not that Nathan wasn't one, but he might leave her on the side of the road if she stared at him all the way to the well-known beach.

'Only since I bought the house. I like being near the sea, and Coogee appealed. Before that I lived on the north shore.' His voice hitched on that last sentence.

'The surfing?' He'd told her he used to surf.

'It wasn't a priority, as I rarely rode the board

at the time. Though that's turned out to be a bonus, like a lot of things about the property. I do hit the waves these days. Besides, the house ticked a lot of boxes and had that wow factor, so I bought it.'

She'd like to see the place sometime. It would tell her a lot about Nathan. Her head nodded forward, and her eyelids drooped shut. Sitting up straighter, she forced her eyelids up and stared out at the road ahead. She'd buy her own home sometime. A small, warm house that would wrap around her; not a sterile mansion that showed off to her friends how wealthy she was. That particular house hadn't been her choice. It'd had Paul written all over the grand frontage, the sweeping staircase, the expansive rooms. The place had felt more like a mausoleum than a home, and as though she as much as the house was on display to all and sundry. 'Not your first property?'

'No. The one I owned first was cosier and more family orientated.' He paused.

Molly waited, hoping she stayed awake long enough to hear what else he had to say.

'I was married. We were hoping to raise our children there. But four years ago it went horribly wrong.'

Wide awake now, she touched Nathan's arm. 'I'm sorry. Life can play nasty when it chooses.'

'You're not wrong there.' Nathan flicked

the indicator and pulled into the outside lane, keeping a safe distance from the truck in front, his fingers tapping impatiently on the steering wheel.

She knew the grief of losing the chance of having a family. It undermined everything she wanted for her future. Unlike her, Nathan could have children if he chose to. Molly returned to watching those fingers as they played a silent, sharp rhythm on the wheel.

'Rosie got ALL.'

Acute lymphatic leukaemia. Molly's heart dropped for Nathan, and his wife. What could she say? No words could help. But a hug might— except hugging Nathan while he was driving along the city highway wasn't conducive to safety. Like her dream? She squeezed his arm softly, and remained quiet for the rest of the ride out to the beach.

Had Nathan told her about his wife in a bid to soften the blow when he asked her about her past? Or were they getting a little closer and he wanted to put it out there straight-up? Yesterday's argument and breakfast seemed a lifetime ago. They'd been scratchy with each other, then friendly to the point he'd had a cup of tea in her apartment. At the time it had seemed a vast improvement in their relationship, and since then she'd exposed the results of her darker side, and he was still happy to spend time alone with her.

Having spent the past two years running solo, to have now shared time talking with a man was hard to take in. It excited her about the future. Seemed she was still capable of mixing and mingling, of having a laugh, of doing things outside her four walls.

'Wakey-wakey.'

A gentle shaking of her arm had Molly sitting up and staring around. 'Sorry.' She never went to sleep in the company of anyone, let alone a man. Another point in Nathan's favour. 'This is Coogee?' The sweeping beach with its golden sand sang to her, reminding her of beach holidays with Gran. Lowering the window, she listened to the waves smacking down on the beach beyond the steps leading down from the street.

'Yes, it sure is.' He glanced along the street, then back at her. 'And, Molly?'

Uh-oh. What had she done? She'd been asleep, couldn't be too serious. 'Yes?'

'Stop saying sorry all the time. Falling asleep isn't a crime. It'd been coming ever since you dropped Burgess in ED. Shock or an adrenaline high does that.'

'I won't get into trouble for throwing him on the floor, will I?' It had only just occurred to her it might be seen as a bad move, she could have endangered others. Not that there'd been any chance of stopping her reaction.

'I'd like to see anyone try to make you out to be the villain. If you hadn't stopped him, Hazel would now have a badly beaten face, at the very least. Believe me, everyone's on your side. The word was going round the hospital within minutes that you stepped up and the question's being asked—where was Security at the time he walked through the doors into the department?'

'He could've gained access by asking to see his wife. He didn't need to get all uptight and angry.' That still would have upset Kath, though.

'Unfortunately you're right. Kath hadn't said she wouldn't see him, and I doubt she would've if asked.' He pushed open his door and unwound his long body to stand upright.

Before Molly had gathered her bag, or her wits, Nathan was opening her door. 'Come on. Let's go and eat.'

She grinned. 'Now you mention it, I'm starving.'

'There's a surprise.' Nathan laughed, and held out a hand to take hers, which he didn't drop as they began walking along the footpath.

For once she didn't try and pull away, or start filling in the sudden shyness swamping her by talking a load of drivel. Instead she looked around at the massive hotel built against the hill, and the row of small shops lining the street heading up the valley. She enjoyed the sense of freedom at being able to hold a man's hand without being frightened, or wary. A warm, strong hand belonging to a caring, exciting guy who was starting to get under her skin in ways she'd long believed wouldn't happen in this lifetime.

Then she let out a sigh. There was no getting away from telling him the bare facts about her past. Nathan had guessed the basics so to go all quiet on him when he was being so darned kind and friendly wasn't right, even when she hadn't told anyone the sordid details since she'd left Perth two years ago. She'd give him an abridged version. Bare facts, and move on.

After they'd eaten.

'Hello, Nathan.' The waitress placed menus before them. 'How's your week been?'

'Hectic, as per usual. Eva, let me introduce Molly O'Keefe. She's a nurse in the department.'

'Hey, Molly, nice to meet you. Are you living around here?'

The girl looked vaguely familiar, which didn't make sense. Unless she lived in the same apartment block as Molly did, but what were the odds? 'Over in Bondi Junction, unfortunately.' She'd love to have an apartment with those views to wake up to every day. It wasn't happening any time soon. Her bank balance couldn't cope.

The money from her half of the marital property was locked in an investment, where it was staying until she decided what to do with it. The money was tainted, as far as she was concerned. Though there was her inheritance from Gran. Hmm. Possibilities started popping up. Her mother would be quick to offer assistance to make up for letting her down in the past, but she'd never ask.

'I know what you mean. It's beautiful around here.' Eva looked at Nathan. 'The usual?'

'You've got steak on the menu?' Molly laughed.

Eva gaped at her. 'Steak? No. The full Aussie breakfast.'

Molly's laugh got louder. 'Do you ever cook your own breakfast?'

'Cook it? Hell, no. Do I tip something out of a cardboard box into a bowl and add milk? Yes, more often than you seem to think.' He grinned before nodding to the waitress. 'Definitely, the works. Molly might take time deciding so can we have a flat white and a long black in the meantime?'

'Coming up.'

As Eva headed across to the barista coffee machine, Molly began scanning the menu. 'I feel I know Eva from somewhere.'

'ED. She came in with burns to her legs after

a cook knocked boiling water off the stovetop and onto her.'

'She was in agony. The head chef came with her, and was so upset you had to calm him down as well.' It had happened during her first week in the department, and she'd been impressed with Nathan's handling of the chef's stress when it was Eva who had needed his attention. 'You helped them both.'

'Later, when the chef had gone, Eva told me the restaurant had a bad safety record and she wasn't going back. I put her in touch with Henri, who owns this place.'

'You did me a huge favour.' Eva placed two coffees before them. 'Molly?'

'Mushrooms on toast, and lots of crispy bacon.'

'Good choice.'

It was. The creamy sauce the mushrooms came in was divine, and the bacon done to perfection. 'I might have to reserve my own table after this.' Molly grinned as she pushed her plate aside and dabbed her lips with a paper napkin. Coogee wasn't so far from Bondi Junction that she couldn't make the trip occasionally to eat scrumptious food, check out those shops and dabble her toes in the sea.

'Help yourself to mine.' Nathan smiled, those

questions back in his eyes now that breakfast was over.

Even knowing how unlikely it was, she'd been hoping he'd let it go. Yet she also thought that by telling him about Paul she'd be testing the water to see how he reacted. It'd be a barometer for the future and how she went about revealing her past to any man she might get serious about. Draining her water, she set the glass down. 'Feel like walking along the beach?' She could not sit here revealing everything, not with him directly opposite and she firmly in his line of vision.

'You read my mind.'

'Oh, no, I didn't.' She could no more read what he was thinking than ride a wave like two surfers were doing out there.

Only three other individuals were on the beach, two in a hurry to get their walk done, probably to head back indoors where it was warmer. Molly zipped her jacket up to her chin.

Beside her, Nathan slipped his hands into his pockets and matched her pace. They were halfway along the beach before she said, 'My divorce came through last Monday. I got the paperwork on Thursday.'

'Was that why you had a toast to yourself at Vicki's breakfast?'

'You noticed?' Was there anything she could

keep from this man? Was that good? Or bad? She'd go for good, with a wary eye.

'I've started observing lots of things about you.' Then Nathan stopped. 'If that sounds creepy, I apologise. It's not meant to. It's only that my opinion of you has changed since yesterday morning.'

She glanced across, and couldn't resist smiling. 'We didn't exactly get off to a great start, did we?' Could be that deep down she'd sensed how he could affect her if she let him near, and so subconsciously she'd been protecting herself by pushing him away. 'Of course we might go back to being grumpy with each other next time we're at work.' Fingers crossed that didn't happen. She liked the man, more than liked, but that emotion was for another day further down the track—if they spent more time together outside the hospital. Nathan had mentioned a car trip. Should she go? It meant making herself vulnerable, if only because he was so considerate towards her, something that still had her defence mechanisms coming to the fore.

'How long were you married?' Nathan brought her back to reality with a bump.

'Two years.' Her voice had taken on an emotionless tone, designed not to give anything away she didn't choose to. 'At first it was wonderful.'

Deep breath, stare at the sand ahead. 'And then it wasn't.'

'I'm sorry to hear that.'

She was sorry she had reason to say it. 'He hit me. Often, towards the end. There was no pleasing him when he was in a mood.'

'I figured that out when you talked about Kath's problem. You understand what she's dealing with.' Nathan came closer, his arm touching hers, his hand now between them—relaxed and there for her. Or so she hoped.

'Every last emotion,' she admitted.

'I hoped I was wrong.' Then he asked, 'Can I hold you?'

She didn't know whether to laugh or cry. Nathan was asking if it was all right to hold her. Pausing in her mad dash along the beach, she faced him square on. 'Yes, please.'

As his arms wrapped around her she became aware of the tension gripping his torso. It didn't frighten her. Again unusual. It only went to show how much she instinctively trusted this man. 'Nathan?'

His forehead rested against hers. 'I am spitting mad. No man has the right to hurt a woman physically. It's appalling.'

'And degrading, and terrifying, and soul destroying,' she whispered.

'Yet you were brave and left him.'

That sounded so simple. Pack a bag and walk out the front door, never to return. Don't look over her shoulder—except she'd been doing that ever since, though not any more. Other than on bad days when she was feeling down.

Nathan continued. 'You're still looking out in case he turns up. At one stage I saw you checking every male that came into the café yesterday.'

She pulled back in his arms to watch the expressions crossing his face. He was angry. For her. The tension eased. No one had done that for her since this appalling situation had begun. Not even the people who should've been there for her. 'He can't. He's locked up for years to come.'

'At least that's good.'

She could get to like this man a lot. Like? Or love? Why not? She was allowed to love again, she just had to get it right next time. 'He escaped once and came after me in Adelaide where I'd moved to get away from the people who thought I'd made it all up. They changed their attitude after the trial, but for me it was too late.' Except for her mum, and that was still a work in progress. 'I tried staying on in Adelaide but there were too many shadows at the corners so I moved here.'

'I'm surprised you can get through a day without checking behind every door in the department and studying each male patient who comes in.' So far Nathan had accepted everything she'd told him without criticism. He'd never understand just how much that meant.

'I used to when I began working at the medical centre in Bondi Junction, but it's exhausting so one day I made up my mind to stop. Not that it happened instantly, but I'm heaps better than I used to be.'

'That says you're comfortable here. Am I right?'

'I'm getting there, and, yes, I want to make a life for myself in Sydney. I will never return to Perth.' Her mother had finally accepted that, right about when she'd acknowledged she'd let her daughter down by not believing her about Paul in the beginning.

Nathan leaned in and his lips touched her forehead, brushed over her skin, before he straightened. 'Good answer. You're one tough lady, Molly O'Keefe.'

The wind gusted sharply, flicking sand at them, and Molly shuddered. From the cold or the memories she wasn't sure. Both, most likely. 'I'm starting to believe that.'

'So you should. I'll say this once, and then I'll keep quiet unless you ever want to talk about it again.' Nathan's hand entwined with hers, and she had no compulsion to pull away. 'You are so brave.' Then he kissed both her cheeks and straightened. 'Let's go find somewhere warmer.'

Molly hadn't told him everything. Nothing about the real possibility she'd never get pregnant again. That was just too close, too painful, to reveal. A huge negative when she was trying to be positive. When they reached his car, she asked, 'Where shall we go now?' She wasn't ready for this to end. She hadn't felt so at ease in years, and it was addictive. She wanted more time with Nathan. Plain and simple. Complicated and interesting.

Nathan looked at her over the roof of his car, a look of disbelief darkening his features as he said, 'I want to show you something.'

Was he sure about that? From the way he was looking at her she thought he was more inclined to take her to the bus station and buy her a ticket out of town. 'What?'

'Wait and see.'

Quick, think of somewhere to take her to. Avoid going home. Because once you show her the self-contained flat you're sunk. There'll be no backing out.

Nathan sucked in chilly air and drove through town, berating himself silently for giving in to the horror with which Molly's story had filled him. Rosie would understand how he had to make sure she was always safe, to protect her from those shadows that haunted her and probably would for a long time to come despite her courageous words. Only then would that beautiful, heart-wrenching smile return more and more readily. A smile that rocked him off his steady stride and woke up parts of him that had been asleep for way too long. Not only his libido, but emotions of longing, caring and wanting to nurture.

Because of that smile he felt as though he'd stepped off the edge of a cliff and had no idea how far below he'd land, or in what condition. Neither did he care.

'No one's said that to me since Gran died. Wait and see,' Molly mimicked in a funny voice. 'Don't be impatient, girl.'

Despite the mire in his head, he laughed. Because Molly made him forget what he'd survived and had him wanting to do whatever it took to get her life back. And his. 'You were close to your grandmother?'

'She was my rock, especially as a child. Believed in me, and taught me a lot about being strong, and not taking for granted everything my mother provided.' Molly hiccupped and turned to stare out the window at the passing scenery. 'If only I'd listened harder before I got married.'

Anger rose in Nathan. Give him ten minutes

with the man who'd done this to her. But it wasn't happening, which was probably just as well. He had to accept she was recovering—without any input from him. He swallowed, flicked the music on, and pointed out some landmarks as he drove.

Molly stared out the window. 'It's a beautiful spot.' A gasp erupted from that soft mouth as he turned onto his street. 'You're taking me to your house.'

No fooling her. 'Yes. If I'm keeping you from getting some sleep then I'm sorry. We don't have to stay long and then I'll run you home.'

If I haven't found another reason for bringing you here apart from the real one.

'I stopped wanting to go to sleep before the mushrooms arrived at the table.'

'Good to know I haven't been boring you the whole morning.' He laughed. Again. See? Molly did that to him. It was scary. Yes, and a little bit fun—exciting, even. Could Rosie have been right when she'd said he would love again? Pulling into his drive, he slowed, braked, and breathed deeply. Who'd have known lungs could ache so sharply when deprived of oxygen? 'This is the back. Come around the front.'

She was quiet as they walked along the pebbled pathway to the fenced edge of his property and looked over the public walkway to the grass area and the ocean beyond. Her silence continued for a good five minutes, making Nathan nervous, though he had no idea why. About to ask her what she was thinking, he hesitated, and was rewarded with a big smile. One of those ones that warmed him from his heart to the tips of his toes, and all places in between.

'It's stunning,' she said with a spark in her eyes he hadn't seen before. 'Truly fabulous.'

Then she might be open to his suggestion. If it was the right thing to offer. Hell, he was nervous. Strange. It wasn't as if he was putting his heart on the line—he was merely helping Molly out. No, he'd been lucky in love once. No one got a second crack at that. Spinning around, he began striding back towards the house. There was no denying, though, that to have Molly in his space meant never getting her out of his head. Did he want to? So much for a challenge. Now he had another one. To love or to walk away while he still could. He stumbled. Damn, but he needed to get a new pair of shoes. These ones were tripping him left and right.

'Nathan? Are you all right?' Molly called from a little way behind him.

'I'm fine,' he replied tersely. 'Come inside.' His alter ego wasn't letting him away with not saying why he'd brought her home. Pressing the numbers to the security system a little too hard, he ground his teeth in frustration. He didn't know if he was coming or going, but helping Molly out was suddenly top of his list. Spontaneity was not one of his strong characteristics, and yet…

At the entrance Molly hesitated, making him feel uncomfortable. His fault. He should have told her straight away why he'd brought her here. 'You mentioned looking for somewhere bigger than your apartment. I have a self-contained flat you might be interested in renting.' There. He couldn't retract it. Heading down the hall, he held his breath. Would she follow? Or would she run out of the house screaming he'd gone too far? No, she wasn't running. Neither was she saying anything. Walking into the flat's living area, he turned to face her. Stunned was the only way to describe her expression. 'Molly?'

'Why would you offer me somewhere to live?'

I have no idea. Except for this strange sensation poking me in the belly—and the chest.

'If you want somewhere temporary, that's fine. Your call.'

Stunned turned to irritated. 'Thanks.' Sarcasm dripped between them. She wasn't looking around, that fierce look he'd only got to know yesterday was back. Worse, her hands were on her hips, fingers tight.

Obviously he wasn't going to be let off the question swinging between them. 'This is going to waste, and if you can use it, why not?' Totally true, just not all the truth.

Her hands dropped away, the fierceness softened.

A return to her good books? He hoped so. He believed more than he could have imagined that he needed her to accept he had her back.

'Thank you,' Molly said. He'd have missed the lifting of her lips if he hadn't been so focused on her. 'I'm a bit surprised. Actually, forget a bit. I'm shocked. I mean, we haven't exactly been the best of friends—until now—yet you're saying I should move into your house?'

'Take a look around, Molly. That's all I'm suggesting.'

And don't ask me anything I'm not prepared to answer—because I don't actually have the answers.

Relief spiralled through him as she wandered away to peek into the double bedroom and then the bathroom, and back to the living room with the kitchen in the corner. At least she was looking. That had to be a good sign. She wasn't about to chop his head off with one of those fast judo moves. He opened the glass doors leading onto the small deck overlooking the sweeping front lawn, which gave the flat a sense of more space than was real. He knew the instant she came to stand beside him, his whole body being on Molly alert.

'It's lovely. And private.'

That had to be a plus, surely? Or maybe not, given her need for security. 'Like I said, I fell in love with this place the moment I set eyes on it and have no regrets.' Nathan looked around and felt happiness swelling in his chest. He'd got it right, and could picture his children running around the lawn one day in the future, when his heart got back to being more than a pump. Something else Rosie had been right about.

'I can see why.' Molly was stalling.

His gut tightened. He *wanted* her to move in. Why? As she'd pointed out, they'd hardly got on until yesterday, their norm not having been overly friendly. Yet in little more than twenty-four hours they had done a complete flip. He'd held her in his arms, caressed her with his lips, held her hand as they'd walked to the café, breathed her scent. And found none of that was nearly enough.

'Come on. You need to see the water up close.' Once again her hand was in his as he strode out, heading back towards the grass strip and sea beyond. Now who was stalling? He did not want to hear her say, no, thanks, and that she'd find somewhere else more suitable to live in her own time.

Damn. He should be grateful if she came out with that. What was wrong with him? A few hours in Molly's company and he acted crazy, inviting her to live in his house and holding her hand like they had something going on. His fingers relaxed their grip on hers and he put a bit of space between them. Tried for sane and sensible. Boring.

'Nathan, do you honestly think it would work with me living here when we're usually on the same shifts in the ED? We'll never get away from each other.'

Go for ordinary, light and friendly. 'You don't think two breakfasts makes us best friends now?'

She stared up at him, those hands back on her hips, this time a hold that didn't indicate her life depended on it, fingers still pink. 'I'm not sure that's what I want.'

'You prefer us being aloof with each other?'

The riotous curls flicked all over her scalp as she shook her head. 'I know you better than that now.' Her mouth lifted, those lips curving seductively. The green in her eyes gleamed like sun on an emerald.

His heart skittered. What the hell? Reaching for her, he brought his mouth to rest on hers, waited in case she didn't want this. When she didn't move away, the need clawing throughout his body won out, and he pressed his lips against hers, and proceeded to kiss her as he'd been thinking of doing since yesterday. Apparently since the day she'd arrived in the ED, if his sense of finally getting somewhere, of the future opening up, was to be believed.

Molly O'Keefe had done a number on him, good and proper. Funny thing was, he didn't give a damn.

CHAPTER SIX

MOLLY FELL AGAINST NATHAN, her breasts pressing into him, her hands wound around his back to feel those muscles tighten under her palms as the kiss deepened. This was Nathan Lupton, and they were kissing. Not any old kiss either, but something that turned her on and made her knees weak and her heart rate go off the scale. She should stop, pull away.

She didn't want to. Couldn't. It was as though they'd been building towards this moment once they'd found themselves sitting together at breakfast yesterday. It was like being stuck in the path of a tornado with nowhere to hide. Not that she wanted to. So much for not trusting people. Except, not once had Nathan made her think he'd ever hurt her. Instead he'd indicated he'd go after anyone who tried to get to her.

This was starting over, getting on with a new life, and if it involved getting closer to a man then she had to take the chance. She was done with stagnating. Why wouldn't she want an exciting man in her life? It wasn't as though she'd been neutered. Everything might have been on hold, yet now the barriers were falling fast, not one at a time, as she'd expected, but crashing at her feet in a pile. Leaning closer, she increased the pressure of her mouth on his and went with the wonderful moment, let the exquisite sensations his kiss created have their way and tease her with yearnings long forgotten.

Now? With Nathan? But was she truly ready for this? She jerked, tugged her mouth free. And didn't know what to say. Words, cohesive thoughts, were as hard to catch as a handful of air.

Nathan's eyes flew open, intense with desire. For her.

Forget trying to think what she might say. Instead, she shivered; a delicious shiver that warmed her skin as it raised soft goose bumps on it. Her arms tightened around him. Why had she stopped kissing him?

'Molly?'

Don't say sorry. 'It's good. I didn't want to stop.' She'd had to, though, or lose control.

'Which, I suspect, is why you did.' His mouth twitched.

'It's too soon.' Regret had her tongue lapping

at her lips, and his eyes followed, causing a knot to form in her stomach.

His nod was slow. 'You're right. It's the same for me.'

'I'd better get going.'

Nathan shook his head. 'Come inside.'

Not to continue kissing. No, he'd agreed they'd moved too quickly, wouldn't expect a rerun of that kiss. She was coming down to earth now. It was unlikely to be comfortable when the kissing was done and they were back to being professional with each other in the department. Though he was fast becoming a friend, if not something more.

You don't kiss friends like that.

Being in Nathan's arms felt safe. Exciting. Nothing like friendship. Also—and this was big—how certain was she that she wanted this after so long denying her needs?

She tramped along beside Nathan, trying to straighten her thinking, getting nowhere except inside his house, where he led her to a sitting room overlooking the lawn and beyond. A large-screen TV dominated one wall, an enormous couch placed strategically in front.

'Take a seat,' he instructed in a voice that said he was about to get serious. Over what? Their kiss?

Please don't. She'd hate that. It would spoil the

moment and hurt, when she'd enjoyed it so much. She didn't need to hear it hadn't been wonderful for Nathan. He could keep that to himself. Talk about out of practice. Gone was the confident girl prior to Paul who used to kiss and leave, or occasionally kiss and stay for the night and then leave. Look at her. She was a blithering wreck because of a kiss. She so wanted to follow up with another, and wasn't going to. She needed to be circumspect. Parking her backside on the edge of the couch, she crossed her legs, folded her arms and waited.

'Whoa, relax, Molly. I'm not about to bite your head off.' He took the opposite end of the couch, and stretched his legs out for ever. Turning in her direction, he eyeballed her. 'Neither am I going to say I regret kissing you.'

Her arms loosened and her hands splayed over her thighs. 'Go on.'

He laughed. 'What more can I say? Other than I'd like to do it again.'

So would she. But—

'But I'm not sure where we're going with this,' Nathan continued. 'I don't know what you expect from men after what's happened to you in the past.'

That makes two of us.

Or did it? Her lungs expanded as she drew a long breath. 'If I hadn't felt comfortable with you it wouldn't have happened.' She'd have backed away, run more like, not leaned in and made the most of Nathan's mouth on hers. 'What happened in the past has to stay there, not taint anyone I get close to in the future. That might sound naïve, but I firmly believe it's the only way to get back a normal, happy life, hopefully with some loving in it eventually.'

'Gutsy comes to mind. How do you do it?'

Fake it till you make it.

'Dig deep for smiles, start trusting those around me, and have fun.'

'Honest too. Though I'm sure there's a lot you haven't told me.' Nathan held his hand up, palm out. 'It's all right. I don't expect you to. All I ask is that you take me seriously, and don't treat me as an experiment to see how you're managing.'

Nathan had been hurt in the past too and wouldn't be rushing to fall in love again. Her eyes widened. 'Now who's being honest?'

'Would you want it any other way?'

This in-depth conversation with a man was foreign—and interesting. 'No. I've never tried to hurt anyone or, to my knowledge, been so thoughtless as to do so. You've got things that upset you too, and I don't want to be the one who reminds you of what you've lost.' A tremor shook Molly. So much for relaxed.

'We've learned a lot about each other in a

short time.' Nathan was studying her, and she felt completely comfortable.

'Which is one reason why I can't move into your flat.' She'd like to get to know Nathan a whole lot better, bit by bit, and that would be best if they weren't living in each other's breathing space. If they were to have a relationship she needed a place to be alone at times while she got used to someone else in her life. Knowing he was on the other side of the wall could encroach on her solitude.

She'd become fiercely independent over the time she'd been alone, and it would take a lot to give up even a little of that. Not even sensational kisses suggesting sensational lovemaking would do the trick. Not yet. Nathan was kind and sincere, or so she believed. While Paul had fooled her with his charm, she doubted Nathan would ever be anything but up-front and caring. But she'd got it wrong once, and that niggled a little.

'Any other reasons for not moving into my flat?'

'We work together.'

'People share living arrangements with work colleagues all the time.' His smile nearly undid her resolve not to give in.

It would take a nanosecond to lean forward and wrap her hand around his arm and bring them closer. Nathan was that damned gorgeous.

The air stuck in her throat. The knot tightened in her belly. She could do this—far too easily. But she hadn't thought it through. She needed to do that first. She was considering it? After the arguments she'd put up moments ago? 'I'm not ready.'

'I'd have your back.'

'I know.' Molly sighed her gratitude. It was true. 'And no one's out there trying to track me down any more. I don't need to check every person who comes within spitting distance.' She believed it, which had to be an improvement on her previous attitude to getting out and about.

Nathan nodded. 'Fair enough. I'm not pushing you to do something you don't want to.'

Settling back into the comfortable, soft, cosy couch, she looked around. A computer sat on a desk in the corner, an up-to-date stereo system in another. 'You've made yourself quite the den, haven't you?' There was a maleness to the sharp white décor with dashes of black in the curtains and the furniture. There was also a loneliness she recognised from her own apartment. The room here was on a far grander scale, but the emptiness felt the same.

'I spend most of my down time in here.' He picked up a remote and pressed some buttons, then music filled the air, a low female voice that lifted the hairs on the back of her neck.

Molly swallowed the urge to sing along. 'Not often, then.' She'd keep digging for info while he was so relaxed with her.

'More than you'd credit me with. I put in a fair amount of time studying and keeping up-to-date with medical programmes and the latest drugs and procedures, even though emergency medicine doesn't change a lot.'

'Why that particular field, instead of, say, surgery or paediatrics?'

'It's when people are most vulnerable. I rise to that. It brings out the best in me.'

'You'd be the same in any area of medicine.'

'True.' He shrugged those eloquent shoulders that she'd held while being kissed. 'There's also a lot of variety in an ED. A bit like a GP practice, I imagine, only lots more cases where there's an urgency about the situation. Sometimes I regret not having the follow-up and knowing how a patient fared long term. At the same time, I don't get to see it all go bad and watch someone I've got to know a little go downhill and have to face the families trying to cope.'

That wouldn't be his thing. Not that it was anybody's. 'You've suffered loss. You'd feel for those patients and their families.' To think this was the man she'd thought irritating and infuriating. He still could be, but now she'd seen behind that mask she'd never accept it at face value again. She might get cross with him but from now on it would take longer to really wind her up. She didn't need to be on guard with Nathan or protective of herself over every word he spoke.

'Yes,' he muttered. 'But then I'm not alone in that.' He stood up, walked to the glass sliding doors leading outside and stared out, his hands on his hips, legs slightly splayed.

She'd gone too far, shouldn't have mentioned his loss. But there was no taking it back. She went to join him, shoulder to shoulder, gazing outward. 'I'm sorry.'

'Do you realise how often you apologise for something?'

'One habit yet to be annihilated.' Sorry hadn't stopped the fists, but she'd always tried.

Pushing a hand through his thick hair, Nathan shook his head. 'Don't be apologetic for what you said. I prefer people don't dodge the issue. I did enough of that all by myself for the first couple of years. Rosie was my life. I cannot deny that, or how what happened has altered the way I go about things now. But I think I'm leading a balanced life again.'

He was ahead of her there, but she was working on catching up fast. 'Receiving my divorce papers knocked down the final block preventing me from getting back on track. I'd been taking baby steps, now I'm ready to take some leaps.'

'Finding somewhere new to live might be one.' He remained staring outside as he continued. 'The offer to move into my flat stands. Despite your arguments, I believe we could make it work just fine. We can talk terms and conditions any time you like.' He was serious, in control of things, but she could do control too.

'The next place I live in will be where I'd like to spend the next few years at least. Permanent, rather than a stopgap.'

'Buy or rent?'

'I haven't given it much thought. I could afford to buy a small house or a bigger apartment in a similar area to where I am now.' That'd mean using the money she'd sworn not to touch, but maybe it was time to let go of that gremlin too. 'I'm not sure where I want to live. There's no hurry.'

'Feel free to run any ideas past me. I've spent all my life in and around Sydney and know where not to buy.'

'Thanks.' Glad he'd dropped the subject of renting his flat for now, Molly headed back to the couch and sank down onto it, smothering a surprised yawn on the way. That was the answer to all this nonsense going on in her head. She was tired from working all night and tossing a man on the floor. She grinned.

I did it. Cool.

Tipping her head back, she stared up at the ceiling and thought, *I really must get going.* She couldn't hang around with Nathan all day. He'd want to catch up on sleep, and probably had plans for the afternoon when he woke up. But it was so comfortable here. She'd take another minute before calling a taxi to take her home.

Nathan woke and raised his hands behind his head on the pillow, stretched his feet towards the bottom of the bed. He'd slept like a baby. His watch showed he'd had nearly four hours. More than enough if he was to get back into his regular pattern tonight.

Was Molly still asleep? She hadn't budged when he'd tucked the blanket around her. It had taken all his self-control not to swing her up into his arms and carry her down to his bedroom so he could lie spooned behind her while they slept. Except there probably wouldn't have been much sleep going on—for him anyway. She flicked every switch he had, and then some.

Who'd have thought it after the way they'd started out? But there was no denying he wanted Molly. She was sexy, sweet, strong, and still recovering from an appalling past. He wouldn't have kissed her for so long but she hadn't stopped, and how was a man supposed to ignore that when the woman fitted perfectly in his arms? Pressed those soft breasts against his chest?

He sat up, swinging his legs over the edge of the bed and leaning his elbows on his knees, then dropped his head into his hands. It had to be a case of wanting what he couldn't have. There hadn't been a woman who'd rattled him like Molly was doing. Not since Rosie. Strange how different they were. Rosie tall, tough, focused; Molly small, soft, trying to be focused on the future and not the past.

A fact that should have him running for the waves. Hadn't seen that coming. All he'd intended was to make her like him. Like? Or desire him? He did want to love again. 'I what?' The question roared across his tongue. 'Yes, I want to love another woman.' Molly?

Leaping to his feet, he crossed to the mirror in the en suite bathroom and stared at the face glaring back at him. Nothing looked any different from what he'd seen last night while shaving before work. He'd been tracking along nicely, and now look at him. Toast. Over a woman he hadn't even liked let alone wanted to kiss at the beginning of the week. Or had he? Had he been in denial all along? Afraid he might actually want to start looking for a future that involved more than himself? Was love possible a second time?

Spinning away from the mirror, he reached into the shower and turned the knob to hot. Cold would be better for what ailed him, but he was a wuss when it came to freezing temperatures; he far preferred the warmth. Even the extreme heat of the outback made him happier than in winter, and Sydney wasn't exactly freezing.

Standing under the water, he knuckled his head. Molly was in there, teasing, taunting with that sassy way she'd used before she'd realised what she was doing. As for her kisses—man, could the woman kiss. His groin tightened just thinking about Molly's mouth on his.

Molly had mentioned baby steps. That's how he needed to approach this. For both their sakes. She might say she was on the road to recovery, but now he knew what to look for he'd seen the sadness, anger and pain in her face and darkening those beautiful eyes at moments when she thought no one was watching. That might go on for a long time even after she found someone to trust and love again.

Like the nights when he still woke to a sodden pillow. Those were rare occurrences now, but they did happen. Rosie would never leave him completely. Likewise, that monster would always be a part of Molly, of who she'd become and where she went from here. But it seemed she was ready to reach out with *him*. He'd better not let her down.

Once dressed in jeans and a navy shirt, he went to see if Molly had woken up.

She was standing in the middle of the kitchen, looking lost. 'So much for calling a taxi. I fell asleep.'

'You needed it.'

'Blame the couch. It's so comfortable.'

When he'd taken the blanket in, Molly had been on her side, her knees drawn up and her hands crossed over her breasts, accentuating their curves and making him wish they knew each better so he could've wrapped her in his arms instead of the blanket. Her face had been relaxed, without the caution that was her everyday approach to people. 'Now you know why I often spend my sleep time there and not in my bedroom.'

'You got any tea?' she asked, then blushed. 'Sorry. I'll get out of here.'

Bet asking that was one of those steps she'd mentioned. 'Tea, coffee, hot chocolate. I've got the works.' He stepped round her and reached inside the pantry.

'Tea, thanks.' Her soft laugh hit him in the gut. 'Cake?'

He winced. 'There's some in here.' He handed

her the box of tea bags and reached for a plastic container. 'This has been in here for a while.' Left by his sister when she'd visited last weekend, the banana cake might be a little the worse for not being eaten.

'You have cake lying around?' She shook her head at him.

'I haven't got a sweet tooth.' Which Allie knew, but still insisted on making him cakes every time she visited, a habit started in the bleak days of Rosie's illness as a way to cheer everyone up. Not that it had worked.

'What a waste.' Molly had the container in her hand. 'The icing's got a distinct blue tinge.'

The disappointment on her face made him chuckle as he slid out the bin so she could dump the cake. 'I've got frozen sausage rolls that won't take too long to heat, if you're starving.' Breakfast had been a long time ago. His stomach was growling quietly, and it wouldn't be long before it got really noisy. He flicked the oven on and opened the freezer.

Again her laughter got to him, tightening one telltale part of his body while softening others. 'How do you keep in such good shape if you're eating things like that?'

'Obviously I don't eat them or that lemon icing would never have had time to change colour.' Molly thought he was in good shape? 'I go for a run most days.' Which paid off in dividends, but he was lucky to have a metabolism that let him get away with quite a variety of delicious foods. Then he looked at her and saw the deep pink shade of her cheeks.

'Yes, right. You know I run too.' She busied herself with tea bags and mugs and getting the milk out of the fridge.

'As well as being into those martial arts.' A picture of Molly dropping that irate man flashed across his mind, tightened his jaw. So much for Security. She should never have been put in that position. She could've been hurt. So could Hazel. 'Your moves looked so easy, as though the man was lighter than a bag of spuds.' His heart had been trying to beat a way out of his chest. Not even seeing Molly had been unharmed had slowed the rate. That'd taken minutes of deep breathing, and pretending all was right in the department once Security finally turned up and removed the guy.

She grinned. 'It was pretty cool, wasn't it? I've worked hard at being able to protect myself, but never has that instinctive reaction taken over to make me do what was necessary. Until now I've only ever thrown a judo partner on the mat, where I get to think about the best throw to make and how to execute it properly.' Her grin slipped. 'It makes me wonder what I'd do if someone on the train or in the street raised an arm to reach for something and I reacted without thinking.'

'I bet it was the atmosphere as much as the man's actions that made you react. We were all tense, him in particular.' Nathan hoped he was right, or Molly would get a complex about something she'd learned for her own protection. Placing the pastries on a tray, he slid them into the oven and slammed the door. 'Ten minutes and we'll be into those.'

'Afterwards, I'll get out of your hair and go home.'

It wasn't his hair she was messing with; it was his mind. 'I'll drop you off. I've got to go to the supermarket anyway.'

Handing him a mug of tea in a steady hand, she nodded. 'Thanks.'

No argument? There was a first. He found the tomato sauce and placed it on the bench alongside some plates. 'Need anything else with your sausage rolls?'

'No.' She sipped her tea while moving to the counter and sitting on a stool, plonking her elbows on the bench with her mug gripped in both hands. Looking around the kitchen made for a large family with its counters and eight-seater table, intrigue filled her gaze. 'Did you furnish the house?'

Darn. One of them was behaving sensibly, and

it wasn't him. Guess she wasn't feeling the vibes hitting him. He got serious, put aside the hot sensations ramping up his temperature. 'The people I bought it off were moving into an apartment in Rose Bay and wanted to start over with decorating and furnishings so I bought some pieces from them, mainly for the bedrooms and in here. While the table's massive, it gets put to good use when my sister and her lot come to stay.'

'Big family?'

'Allie's got four kids, and a very patient partner. She's like an Energizer battery, no stopping her. She wears everyone out.'

Molly was smiling. 'She sounds like fun.'

'I think you'd like her. And the other two and their broods.' He was getting ahead of himself. Molly did not need to meet any of his family. Not yet, anyway.

'You've got three sisters?'

'Yep.' He jerked the oven door open. 'Let's eat.'

Then he'd take her home before going for a run to work out the kinks in his body put there by being too close to Molly. Nathan muttered an oath under his breath. He had this bad. 'You got plans for the afternoon?'

'Not a lot. Groceries, washing, a run, do the crossword, wash my hair.' She grinned.

'Sounds action packed.' He grinned back. 'Phone me if you're stuck for a word.'

Then her eyes lit up. 'Actually, I think I'll go watch a game of basketball.'

CHAPTER SEVEN

A<small>FTER A QUICK</small> shower Molly dressed in fitted black jeans and a pink jersey that deliberately did not match the red curls she attacked with a hairbrush, then followed up with styling gel that did nothing to tame the wildest of them. With a shrug she selected a black leather jacket from the array in her wardrobe. It had been years since she'd worn anything bright pink, and she felt great. Never again would anyone tell her to get changed into something that toned down her complexion. No one.

Halfway out the door she turned back and snatched up the sports bag at the back of her wardrobe. Chances were it would languish in her car, but she was feeling lucky so she might as well go prepared. Humming was another first as she made her way down and outside to where her car sat in a massive puddle by the kerb. Thank goodness for her red, thick-heeled, soft-as-down leather ankle boots. Not only did they look gorgeous but they could keep water at bay without tarnishing the leather.

Grr, grr. The engine gave a metallic groan. Molly turned the ignition off, counted to four, tried again. Bingo. The motor coughed but kept going. She had power. Perfect. She really needed to start it at least every second day if she was going to leave the car out in the weather. Where else could she park it? The apartment didn't come with an internal garage. Or any designated place for vehicles.

Wind rocked the car as she drove away. Hunching her shoulders so her chin was snug against her turtleneck jersey, her humming turned to singing a cheerful song she'd sung often back in the days she'd been truly happy, getting louder with every corner she turned. By the time she reached the indoor sports arena her jaws were aching and a smile was reaching from ear to ear. Hot damn. That was the first time she'd sung her favourite song in years.

Going to watch the Roos team she'd been a part of until two months ago had been a brainwave. They were playing against one of the strongest teams in the local competition, the odds slightly in their favour. She began to hurry. The game had started ten minutes ago and she hated to miss any more. The idea to come here had arrived out of the blue, but with every passing moment it seemed better and better. Catching up with the women she'd played with, and hopefully making up for being so remote whenever they'd tried to get her to join in the after-match sessions in a nearby bar, had become imperative if she was to keep getting up to speed with her new life.

Inside the stadium she searched out the coach and reserves sitting on the benches, watching the game. 'Hello, Coach. Mind if I sit with you to watch the game?'

Georgia flipped her intent gaze from the team to her, and tapped the chair beside her with her notebook. 'Get your butt down here, girl. Where've you been?'

'Hey, Molly, how are you?'

'Molly, I tried to get hold of you to come to a party last month.'

'Hi, how's that new job going?'

'I'm great. I'll give you my number. The job's wonderful.' Wow. No knots of anxiety needed loosening. Everyone was friendlier than she deserved. Sinking onto the seat, she looked around. 'I see you trashed the Blue Heelers last week.' It was the one team everyone had believed might knock them off the top of the leader board.

'Annihilated them.' Coach laughed. 'Glad you're keeping up with us.'

'First thing I look for in the local news on

Monday mornings. I miss you guys.' More than she'd realised. When she'd played for the team she'd focused on not letting anyone close, afraid they'd let her down if she needed them in any way, as her friends back in Perth had when it had come out about what had been happening. In the end, staying with the team, not going out for drinks after a game or attending the barbecues that they had once a month, not getting involved as everyone else did, had got hard to face, which in turn had exhausted her, so she'd left.

'You chose to leave.' Coach never minced her words.

'I did.' Molly turned to watch the game on the court. 'How's Sarah doing?' The girl who'd replaced her had spent four weeks on the bench after breaking a wrist in a particularly tough match but had resumed playing a fortnight ago.

'Back to her usual Rottweiler attitude and earning us points to boot. I think the wrist still gives her grief, but I'm the last person she'll admit that to.'

'No one likes telling you anything that might give cause to be sat on the bench for a game.'

'That why you left?' Georgia was watching the game, writing shorthand notes in the notebook, but she wouldn't miss a breath, word or a movement Molly made.

'I felt crowded.'

'Being part of a good, functioning team means being in each other's pockets at times.'

'I wasn't ready for that.'

'You kept to yourself a lot.'

Modus operandi. It had worked. It had kept her safe and—lonely. 'Can't deny that.' Her eyes were on the ball as Emma threw it to Sarah, who lobbed it into the net. 'Go, Roos. Good one, Sarah.' Molly leapt to her feet, stabbing the air with her fists, left, right, left, right. 'You beauty.'

Georgia was calmly making notes. 'Never seen you fly out of your skin before.'

Molly sat back down, a grin on her face. How had she not got all excited over being a part of this team? When she'd played for the under eighteens in Perth she'd been the loudest, most enthusiastic member of the team. Today it seemed she really might be getting her life back. Her grin widened as relief soared.

'Guess you didn't know me very well.' Hell, she hadn't realised how far down the ladder she'd dropped. Yet all of a sudden she was here, getting out and *looking* for fun, not just hoping it might come her way if someone had time to spare for her. When she'd determined to get out and start living she hadn't expected it to happen so fast. It was Nathan. By believing in her, he'd pushed her boundaries and helped her open up some more. 'I'm adept at keeping hidden in plain sight.'

Past tense, Mol. You're over that now.

Georgia's gaze was on every move happening on the court. 'I figured.'

Coach was the second person she'd opened up to, though only briefly. There'd been no in-depth talk about Paul and the abuse, but just admitting she had problems had been huge and had felt good in a way she'd never have believed.

It was good the barriers were dropping here too, but there were some she wouldn't let go. The likelihood of infertility for one. Today Nathan had learned more than she was prepared to share with just anyone. She'd spent so long trying to make people believe she was being abused it was hard to let go of the reticence to talk about it now. What if she woke up tomorrow to find it was all a load of bulldust and she wasn't any further on? That people thought what happened was her own fault?

Then you'll try again, and again, until you get it right. Until people accept you for who you are.

Nathan hadn't laughed or told her she was attention-seeking. No, he'd believed her from the get-go. Her grin had slipped, so she dug deep for another and found it wasn't as hard to do as it used to be.

Molly focused on the game.

The score was twenty-seven all.

The opposing team called for a substitute.

Coach stood up. 'Eloise on. Carmen off.'

At half-time the team swilled water from bottles, wiped faces with towels, crowded around Coach for instructions, and said hi to Molly as though she'd never been away.

The third quarter got under way, and the score continued to climb, each team matching the other, the Roos getting ahead only to have the Snakes catch up and pass them, before they took back the lead.

Sarah snatched the ball, blocked an opposition player and swung around to throw for a goal, and tripped over the other player's foot. Down she went, hard, her elbow cracking on the floor, reaching out with her other hand to prevent hitting the deck with her head. Pain contorted her face as she cried out, pulling her wrist against her midriff.

The coach's expletives were the more damning for being spoken quietly. 'That's the last thing Sarah needs. To do her wrist in again.'

Molly rushed on court with Georgia and knelt down beside Sarah. 'Tell me where the pain is.'

'Same place as last time.'

'Where you fractured it?'

Sarah nodded abruptly, her lips white. 'Yeah.'

'Can I take a look?'

Another nod, and Sarah pushed her arm towards her. 'It feels just the same as before. It's broken again.'

Molly carefully touched the rapidly swelling wrist, then felt up Sarah's arm and over the hand. 'Okay, I agree with you. We need to get you to the emergency department.'

A first-aider sank down on his knees beside them. 'Let me look at that.'

Georgia glared at the young man. 'Molly here's an emergency nurse, and she thinks Sarah has broken her wrist. I'll take her word on it.'

'All right, then. We need to get her to hospital.' Molly stood up. 'I'll take her.'

Sarah glared at them. 'I'm not going anywhere until the game's finished. I want to watch the last quarter.'

'That's not a great idea. You're in pain,' Molly said.

'You're telling me?' The woman's eyes widened. 'I know what the damage is, know how the pain works, and I can deal with it for a little while longer. Now, help me off the court so the game can resume.'

Molly smiled at her courage as she took an elbow and Georgia put an arm around her waist. 'You're one tough cookie.'

'Better believe it,' Sarah said, then gasped

with pain. Locking eyes on Molly, she growled, 'Don't say a word.'

'Okay.' But she wanted to bundle her up and rush her to an ED to get painkillers on board.

Once they had Sarah settled on the bench, and the game was under way again, Georgia leaned close to Molly. 'I don't suppose you've got some sports shoes with you?'

Her heart thumped once, loud and hard. 'Yes. But I'm out of practice.'

'You still run every day?'

'Yes. What about the other players?' The ones who turned up every week all season.

Standing up, Georgia growled, 'Don't you want us to win this game?'

That was one mighty compliment. 'Back in a minute.'

Shorts and a shirt in the bright yellow team colour were shoved into her hands. 'Put these on while you're at it.'

'Bottoms up.' Eloise raised her glass and tipped the contents down her throat, and most of the other team members followed suit.

Molly sipped her sparkling water. It tasted like the best champagne out there. They'd won. She'd scored eight points. Unreal.

'Glad you dropped by,' Georgia muttered beside her. 'But don't think you're getting out of Wednesday night practice from now on.'

So she was back on the team, whether she liked it or not. Thing was, she *loved* it. *And* this getting together with everyone. Once, she'd gone out of her way to avoid it; now she felt like she belonged with these women. 'One problem. I'm on shift this Wednesday night from three to eleven.'

'Some of the girls are working out here tomorrow at nine. Don't be late.'

'Yes, boss.'

'Better believe it.' Georgia winked. Then pulled her phone from her pocket. 'Sarah's texted. She's having surgery tomorrow. That'll put an end to her playing for the rest of the season.'

'Unfortunately you're probably right.' A second fracture on top of the previous one was not good. Molly felt her phone vibrate in her pocket. 'Nathan' showed up on the screen. Her heart went flip-flop. He was the last person she'd expected to hear from, despite their harmonious morning. 'Hi. How's things?'

'I saw your car parked downtown and thought I'd see what you were up to, if you'd like some company. But...' and he chuckled '...it sounds as though you're in the middle of a party.'

'I'm at the Lane Bar with the Roos basketball team. I used to play for them.'

Played for them today and made some points. Yeeha.

'Feel free to join me. Us.' He wouldn't come. She'd been rash suggesting it. 'Some of the others' partners are here.'

'Two minutes.' Gone.

She stared at the phone. Had that really just happened? Nathan was coming to have a drink with her? Her heart raced.

You did kiss him this morning. Maybe he wants another.

He could get as many kisses as he wanted from most single females he crossed paths with. He was drop-dead gorgeous and damned nice with it. Nice? Okay, kind, considerate, opinionated and bumptious. But if he made to kiss her again then she wasn't saying no. Yeah, well. She sighed. The kiss had been pretty darned awesome. Her knees still knocked thinking about it.

That might be exhaustion from charging around the court, not desire, Mol.

Sipping her drink, she stifled a yawn. It had been a long, emotional roller-coaster of a day and suddenly she felt shattered. Just when Nathan was about to join her.

One good thing about Molly's red hair was she was easy to find in a crowd. Another—maybe not so good?—she drove him wild with need, but that was on hold as he tried to slow down his pursuit of her. Yeah, right. If that was so, why was he here? The challenge had got out of hand fast, to the point he didn't know who was challenging who. Hopefully Molly was unaware she rocked him off his usually steady feet.

He stood watching her for a moment as she chatted with the women surrounding the table they stood at, her finger running down her cheek as she laughed over something someone said. This was a whole new Molly from the one he thought he knew in the ED. Yet the vulnerability was still there in the guarded way she stood, one shoulder slightly turned, ready to spin around if she sensed trouble approaching.

'Hey, Molly,' he called, a little louder than necessary, not wanting to disturb her comfort zone.

The curls flicked left then right as her head shot up and around. The smile spreading across her mouth hit him hard in the belly. 'Hey, you, too.' She shuffled sideways to make room for him.

Nathan stepped up beside her, happy when she leaned his way so that their arms touched. 'Looks like you're all celebrating.' He nodded at the array of glasses on the table.

Her smile extended into a grin. 'We won.

Against the hardest team we have to play all season.'

'We? You played?' Hadn't she said she was going to *watch* a game?

'Since Coach knew me she asked if I'd fill in for the last ten minutes after one of the girls broke her wrist. Re-broke it.'

'Why did you leave in the first place?'

Molly's look told him to shut up, so he did, for now.

'What Molly's not telling you is that she scored eight points,' one of the women said in a very loud voice.

Molly shook her head. 'It was a team effort. Nathan, let me introduce everyone.' She went around the table, stumbling when it came to naming the men and laughing when they teased her about her memory. 'This is Nathan Lupton, a—a friend of mine.' Colour filled her cheeks. 'We work together.'

She didn't have a definite slot to fit him into. Friend, colleague. What else? He had no answer either. 'Can I get you a drink?' He needed a beer, fast, before he came up with some whack-a-doo ideas and put them out there.

Molly shook her head. 'No, thanks. I'm good.'

'Be right back.' *Don't go anywhere.* Luck was on his side. The bar was momentarily quiet, no doubt a hiatus in a busy night. 'Thanks, mate.'

He took his beer and handed over some cash before returning to his reason for being there.

She was toying with her glass. 'I was struggling with fitting into the group. On court, fine. Off court, not so good.'

Nathan nodded. 'Same as you've been with your workmates. I'm picking same reasons too.'

'Yes. At least I'm doing something about it now.' Her eyes met his. 'Were you headed somewhere in particular when you saw my car? How did you recognise it, by the way? It's so ordinary even I have trouble finding it in a parking garage.'

'I wasn't a hundred percent certain. That's why I gave you a buzz instead of checking out the bars first. How long have you been here?' Molly looked tired, and her eyes were a little glassy. Too many of those bubbly wines that she seemed to be enjoying? That on top of last night's shift, and only a few hours' sleep today, would knock anyone off their perch.

She glanced at her watch, and gasped. 'It's after ten? I think we got here around five thirty. No wonder I'm zonked.' Then she glanced at him, and guilt filled those eyes. 'Sorry. That's rude when you've just arrived. We had a celebratory drink, then a meal and some more drinks. Everyone's stoked to have won. I'm going to the training session tomorrow morning since I can't make Wednesday night practice. I'll probably ache in places I don't know I've got afterwards.' She drained her glass and dropped it back on the table with a thud. 'Damn, I'm talking too much.'

'Yes, but it beats the cold shoulder routine.' He smiled to show he wasn't looking for trouble. 'I like the Molly I'm getting to know.'

She stared at him.

'What? Have I grown a wart on my nose?'

'Not quite.' Finally she dropped her eyes to focus on her hands clasped together in front of her.

'Molly?'

She blinked, sighed, looked at him again, this time with remorse clouding her expression. 'Thank you for not running a mile when I told you everything this morning.'

Oh, Mol. 'As if I'd do that.' Nathan lifted one of her hands and wrapped his fingers around it.

'I knew you wouldn't before I told you or I wouldn't have said a word. It was blatantly clear you'd have my back right from the moment I tossed that creep onto the floor. Actually, I think I'd already reached that conclusion before then.'

'So what's the problem?'

'I probably haven't got one that a good night's sleep won't fix.'

'Then let's go.'

Her curls flicked. 'You just got here.'

'I can leave just as quickly. Come on.'

A tight smile flitted across her mouth. 'Okay. Sorry, everyone, but I'm heading home. I'm knackered.'

'Yeah, yeah.' Someone laughed. 'Your man turns up and suddenly you're tired. We get it.'

Heat spilled into Molly's cheeks, but she didn't give one of her sharp retorts. Instead she managed a quiet, 'Whatever,' and slung her bag over her shoulder to walk out of the bar, her hand still firmly in Nathan's.

On the footpath Molly turned right.

Nathan tugged her gently to the left. 'My car's this way.'

Pulling her hand free, she nodded. 'Mine's the opposite way, as you must know if you saw it parked.'

'I'll give you a lift.'

Those curls moved sharply. 'I'm fine. I need my car in the morning.'

Okay, now he had to be brutal. 'Molly, you've been drinking. You cannot drive.'

Her mouth fell open. Her eyes widened. Then she found her voice. 'You think I'm drunk?' she screeched.

'Yes, I do. You said you've been in the bar for hours. Drinking was mentioned.' No way was she getting behind the wheel of her car. 'Your eyes are glassy and you were talking the hind leg off a rabbit in there.' He jerked a thumb over his shoulder in the direction of the bar. 'Which is unlike you.' Unless she was nervous, but he didn't believe her nerves had anything to do with this.

'You're wrong.' She spun away to storm down the road.

'Molly.' He caught up with her. 'Please be sensible and let me take you home. It would be safer for everyone.'

She stopped so abruptly he had to duck sideways to avoid knocking into her. 'I had one alcoholic drink when we first arrived. Since then I have been downing sparkling water by the litre. I am not a danger to anyone.'

'Right.' Even to him his sarcasm was a bit heavy as he stepped in front of her.

Stabbing his chest with her forefinger, she glared at him, the anger ramping up fast in those wide eyes. 'I am tired. Not drunk. Please get out of my way. Now.'

'Even exhaustion is a good reason not to drive.' Lame, but true. And desperate. He didn't want her driving. Giving her a lift would make him happy. Apparently not her. He should let this go, but deep inside was a clawing itch that made him try harder to win her over. Reaching for her hand, he tried to pull her in the opposite direction.

She jerked free, stretched up on her toes and said in the coldest voice he'd ever heard, 'Out of my way, Lupton. Damn, but you're so cocky and infuriating.'

When he didn't move she stomped around him and continued down to her car, head high, boots pounding the tarmac. 'I'll follow you,' he called, and headed for his vehicle so as not to lose her. He was going to make sure she got home safely, one way or another.

Cocky and infuriating. What the hell was that about? Putting him in his place? He'd laugh if it didn't sting. Here he'd been thinking they were getting somewhere. Into a deep, murky hole at the moment.

Slamming the stick into drive, he pulled out and caught up to her at the lights. So he'd infuriated her. No surprises there.

He'd insisted she get into his car.

He hadn't listened to her when she'd said she hadn't been drinking.

He had tried to force his opinion on her.

Starting to sound like her ex.

One very big difference. He would never, ever, use his fists. Molly knew that, or she wouldn't have gone to his house with him that morning. Wouldn't have fallen asleep on his couch, leaving herself vulnerable.

She might not have kissed him either. Keeping a respectable distance, he followed Molly's car to her apartment.

He owed her an apology for being such a prat.

Even if he still thought she should've come with him, he had to say sorry. This argument was bigger than what he'd wanted her to do. It was about not believing her, not letting her make her own decisions—in other words, control. He didn't do control, unless it was about himself. People were allowed to make their own mistakes, unless they endangered someone else in the process. Unfortunately he didn't want Molly making a hideous mistake and so he'd overreacted. She'd had her share of bad deals. She didn't need any more.

Now he had to find a way back into her favour.

Molly closed her door with a firm click, leaned back against it and stared up at the ceiling. 'Damn you, Nathan. Your bossy manner had me reacting faster than a bullet train.'

Her bag slid off her shoulder and hit the tiles with a bang, making her jump. She was wired. And cold. Driving home with her window down to blast the tiredness and keep her alert had chilled her while her temper had combated some of the cold. Now both were backing off. She'd let Nathan get to her—again. Back to how it'd always been between them before birthday breakfasts and judo throws and spilling the beans about her past. It might be for the best. If she hadn't kissed him and been kissed back. Because now she wanted more. Lots more. If she could forgive him for believing she was drunk—*and* telling her what to do.

Picking up her bag, she headed to the kitchen and the kettle. A cup of tea was supposed to remedy lots of things. Hopefully her indignation was one of them.

The buzzing doorbell echoed through the apartment. 'Molly, it's me. Nathan,' he added in his don't-fool-with-me attitude. 'I want to talk to you.'

Well, guess what? She didn't want to talk to him. Filling the kettle, she pushed the 'on' button.

'I know you're in there.'

Who let him into the building this time? Seemed he charmed everyone he came across. Except her. No, even her, when she stopped trying to resist him.

Buzz. Knock, knock. 'Molly.'

Persistent. No surprise there. Back to the door, growling into the speaker, 'Go away, Nathan. I have nothing to say to you right at this moment.'

Except that you've upset me, and stirred me in ways a man hasn't in a long time.

'You want me to shout until the neighbours come out to see what's going on?'

'Go for it.' She huffed at the peephole.

'Let me in.'

Definitely louder, and he wouldn't stop there. Another huff and she wrenched the door wide. 'You're not coming in.'

'Fine.' He leaned a shoulder against the door-jamb and concentrated his entire focus on her.

The cheek of him, so damned sure of himself. She stabbed his chest before she put her brain in gear and jerked her hand away. 'You think you can say what you like to me and get away with it.'

'Wrong, Molly. I know I'll never get away with anything around you.'

Her mouth dropped open. Hurriedly closing it, she swallowed hard. What did he say?

'You don't take any bull from anyone and, for some reason, especially from me.' His mouth twitched. 'I like that.'

Again her jaw dropped. Again she slammed it shut, jarring her teeth in the process. This wasn't going according to plan. Not that she'd had one other than to keep Nathan out of her apartment. 'Right. Fine. You've had your say so kindly remove yourself from my doorway so I can close the door.'

He didn't move a centimetre. 'I haven't told

you why I'm here.' His eyes were locked on her as though seeing right inside to every thought crossing her confused mind. 'Can you spare me a couple of minutes?' That couldn't be a plea. Could it? His eyes were dark, his mouth soft.

Nathan was making it hard to stay uptight and focused when he looked at her like that. This was probably the biggest mistake she'd made in a while, but she stepped back, holding the door wide, and nodded, once, abruptly.

'Thanks.'

The tenderness in his gaze made her shiver. Had he done an about-face? If so, why? No, he wouldn't have. Molly headed into her lounge, where she remained standing. To sit would give him a height advantage. The kettle whistled, clicked off. She ignored it.

Nathan stood before her, not so close as to dominate her but near enough that she was fully aware of him. Heck, she was aware of him all over the ED, so there was no way she could ignore him in her apartment even if she shut herself in the bathroom.

He reached for her hands and said, 'I'm very sorry for doubting you. I had no right to do that. Or to criticise you. If I could take those words back, Molly, they'd be gone already. Not thrashing around inside your head.'

He understood her too well. Now he'd stunned

her. Nathan Lupton had said sorry—to her. The tension fell away, leaving her wobbly, with a spinning head and racing blood. Somehow her fingers had laced with Nathan's. 'Accepted,' she whispered. What else could she do? Being offside with Nathan wasn't what she wanted. Not now, not ever if possible.

His gaze remained fixed on her. The coffee shade of his eyes had lightened to tan with hints of green and black. A smile was growing on his lush mouth.

Heat expanded in her stomach, spreading tentacles of longing throughout her body, knocking at her heart, shimmering into her womanhood, weakening her knees.

'Molly?' Nathan's hands took her face to ever so gently bring her closer to his mouth. Those full lips brushed her quivering ones, apologising and teasing. Then he pulled back to again lock eyes with her. Heat sparked at her, set her blood humming, lifting her up on tiptoe.

As her mouth touched his she fell into him, winding her arms around to spread her hands over his back, pushing her awakened nipples against his solid chest. She breathed deeply. *Nathan.* His name reverberated around her skull, teasing, laughing, giving.

Oh, yes, giving. His mouth was devouring hers, his tongue plunging deeper with every lick.

Hands skimmed over her arms, her waist, then held her butt tenderly while stroking, firing her up to the point of no return. Molly hesitated, her mouth stilled. Did she want this? Stupid question. Her mouth went back to kissing him hard, demanding more, sharing everything.

Then Nathan raised his head. 'Molly?' Disappointment knocked behind her ribs when he took her hands and held them tightly between his. 'I think I'd better go while I still can.'

Thump, thump went her heart. He was right. The next step would be in the direction of her bedroom, and despite feeling comfortable and safe with Nathan, she wasn't as ready as that entailed. Sure, they could make out and have fun, but the sun would rise and then she'd have plenty of misgivings to deal with. This man had got closer to her than anyone in a long time, but it had happened so fast she needed to pause, take a breath, and think about what she wanted. 'You're right. It's too soon for me.'

He squeezed her hands gently, brushed his lips across hers, and stepped back. 'Me, too.'

CHAPTER EIGHT

MOLLY WAS WHACKED. Every muscle ached, and she'd thought she was fit. Lifting the kettle to fill it took energy she didn't have. That afternoon's basketball game had been tough. She'd worked hard to justify Coach's belief in her. They'd barely won—surprising considering the opposition team was ranked seventh compared to their second slot in the competition.

Pride lifted Molly's spirits further. Not once had she failed to take a catch or run the length of the court bouncing the ball. She'd made most of her shots count, taken some intercepts without too much difficulty. Yes, it had been a good game, and now she was worn out.

Work had been busy beyond normal all week, making everyone tired and scratchy. Though Nathan had remained friendly and easygoing with her. There'd been no more kisses or time together away from work, but lots of laughs and friendship. A very normal week for most people, and she couldn't ask for more.

Her bed looked so tempting since she'd changed the sheets and straightened up her room. The washing machine was humming in the kitchen, the pantry had some new food on the shelves, and her newly washed hair was under control. Not that that would last, the curls being the unreliable nuisances they were.

Sinking on the edge of the bed, there was no holding back the smile splitting her face. Or the soft, warm feeling settling over her. Yes, it seemed she was getting up to speed with returning to a normal life, and she had Nathan to thank for some of it. That man made her feel special. She only hoped she'd given some of the excitement and wonder back.

Without thought, she sprawled over the bed, her head snug on her pillow as she kept running images of Nathan through her mind. Laughing over something silly, stitching up a cut in an old man's arm, kissing her. They were more than friends now. But were they becoming a couple? Hardly.

The ringing phone woke her. Scrabbling around the top of her bedside table, her fingers latched onto the instrument just as the ringing stopped. Damn.

Then it started again. Nathan's name blinked out at her.

'Hi.' She scrubbed the sudden moisture from her eyes. It was *only* a phone call.

'Hey, Molly. How did the game go?'

Man, she loved that voice. Over the phone it was even more gravelly. 'It was awesome. We won.'

'So you'll be out celebrating. Though it does sound rather quiet.'

'I'm at home. Some of the girls were going to a wedding and the rest of us had other things to do.' She hadn't, but she'd fallen in with the general consensus that one weekend not celebrating wouldn't hurt.

'Bet you're exhausted. But I was wondering if you're up to meeting my mob. They've descended upon me without warning, and I need some backup.'

'You didn't know your family was coming to visit?'

Nathan's laugh was a short hoot. 'The day any of my sisters tell me they're on their way I'll buy a lotto ticket. All the nieces and nephews are here too, I might add.'

'How many?' Nathan wanted her to meet these people? Seemed they were way past being civil with each other and on to greater things.

'Eight.'

'You're pulling my leg,' she spluttered.

'Nope.' He laughed. 'Three married sisters make for eight brats to buy birthday and Christmas presents for.'

It didn't sound like he resented that. Quite the opposite. He seemed very happy he belonged to this family. 'You must have lists everywhere to keep up with what you've bought who, and what you'll get them next.'

'You have no idea. So, are you up for them? I have to be fair and warn you it won't be a quiet afternoon and you'll never have seen a meal like it. Also, dinner will be at some ridiculously early hour that's closer to lunch so that everyone can be back on the road early. Getting the ankle-biters home late causes bedlam the next morning apparently.'

'It doesn't sound as though any of this is a hardship.' Did he really want to introduce her to his family? Had he thought it through? *Grab the opportunity.* Even if they didn't go much further with whatever was happening between them, she should get out and enjoy herself while she could. 'I could come for a few minutes,' she teased. This teasing was another first. She'd forgotten how to long ago—safer that way—but apparently the ability had been hovering under the surface.

'Minutes? Oh, no, you don't. All or nothing, girl.'

She laughed. This was so different from anything she'd have expected from Nathan before Vicki's breakfast. Before V day and after V day were now her measures. 'I'm on my way. Well, I will be when I've spruced myself up a bit.'

'Don't get carried away. By the time the little horrors have finished with you you'll wish you'd saved yourself the effort.'

'This sounds like fun.'

'You have no idea.' Nathan was laughing fit to bust as he hung up.

Eight kids in one hit? Crikey. Molly stared around her cramped bedroom. What was happening to her? She'd been out more often to more places since V day than at any time throughout the last two months put together. Even better, she was happy. The only time she hadn't been was when Nathan had accused her of being drunk, and his apology more than made up for that.

Leaping off the bed, she threw the wardrobe door open. What to wear? Something to impress Nathan, even if he had warned her to downplay the outfit?

Molly settled for tight black jeans, a cream jersey, and her favourite red boots. No, cream was a magnet for grubby hands. Tossing that jersey aside, she flicked hangers from one side to the other, found the bright orange jersey and tugged it over her head, instantly feeling at ease. Orange top and red curls. Perfect. Lipstick. Red or orange? Red was the first one to land in her hand, so red it was. She had to stop singing to apply the gloss.

So much for exhaustion and muscle aches. She was going to a party of sorts. Bring it on.

Nathan's house on Saturday morning had had an air of quiet elegance about it, with the sweeping lawns and ocean view attention grabbing.

Today Molly felt as though she'd dropped into the middle of a circus. Who knew kids could make so much noise? Then there was the exuberant adult joining in all the games and flying kites and chasing balls, seemingly all at once. Gone was any vestige of Dr Lupton.

'Hey, you came.'

'You didn't think I'd turn up after saying I would?'

'I figured you'd pull into the drive, hear the racket going on and take off faster than a rocket.' Nathan wrapped an arm around her shoulders. 'I've said it before—you're one brave lady. Come and meet the tribe. I promise not to quiz you on names later.'

She felt a bit bedazzled as she was introduced to sisters, brothers-in-law and all those children, and had to pinch herself to make sure this was real. It was nothing like her family, where she was the only child, with her mother and all the expectations of grandeur and a father in New Zealand replaced by a stepdad. They loved her, but this? She looked around and swallowed. The Luptons left her speechless. It was probably just as well or she might say something so odd they'd be putting her back in her car and waving good-bye before she'd had time to relax.

'Here, get this into you.' One of the women handed her a glass of wine. Annemarie? Or Jessie? It wasn't Allie, or was it? 'I hope you like wine, because a few hours with us will turn anyone to drink. We're enough to scare off the bravest.'

Molly accepted the glass. 'I think you might be right.'

'Try and leave, and I'll wheel-clamp your car,' Nathan called over his shoulder as two young boys tried to tackle him to the ground. 'And that's Annemarie.'

She laughed. She was doing a lot of that lately. Again Nathan had seen right through her confusion. 'Thanks, Annemarie.' Colour filled her cheeks. 'I'm in the mood for a wine, which is rare.' So much had been happening, so something, someone to relax with was perfect. Her gaze found Nathan. Having a drink made standing around talking to strangers easier, and kept her hands busy. Unless— 'You look like you need some help,' she called over to Nathan.

'Stay back, and look after those sore muscles. We have a few hours to get through yet.' When she lifted one eyebrow, he laughed. 'You're walking round like a toddler on a high.' Boys and girls fell onto Nathan, pushing him onto the lawn, tickling him as he carefully tossed one after another into the air and caught them again.

'Let's sit on the sidelines,' Annemarie said, heading for the expansive deck and some chairs, sheltered from the light, cool breeze coming off the sea. 'The men can play while the women relax with wine and nibbles. It's tiring just watching.'

Settling into a wicker chair, Molly watched Nathan and his brothers-in-law chasing kids and balls around the lawn and waited for the questions from the sisters, sipping her wine in an attempt to look the part of a friend with nothing else to do on a Saturday afternoon. That part was kind of true. When the grilling didn't come she began to enjoy herself.

'Mum, when can we eat? I'm hungry.' A little girl stood in front of them a while later, hands on hips, just like her uncle Nathan had been doing earlier.

'Ask Uncle Nathan. He's in charge of the barbecue.'

'Now,' came the call.

The women hit the kitchen, and Molly found herself taking an endless supply of salads, breads, dressings and sauces out to the huge table in the conservatory. Delicious smells wafted from the barbecue where Nathan and the guys had begun cooking steak and sausages.

'How're you doing?' Nathan came over to her. 'I've neglected you a bit.'

'It's fine. I don't need to be babysat. Anyway, I liked talking with your sisters.'

'That's a worry.' He grinned.

'You were having fun with the kids. You're just like them, getting muddy rolling around on the lawn. I half expected you to ask for a turn on the trolley.' There was a box on wheels that the men had taken turns pulling children around in.

'No one would take me on.' Another grin.

'I can see why your family descends on you.' No sign of being in control or wanting things done his way today. 'You love those kids and they love you back just as much.' She could see him with a large family of his own. Not with her—she couldn't. Her stomach squeezed a little, her mouth lost the sweet taste of the wine. 'You ever plan on having your own brood?'

Nathan turned from watching the kids arguing over a game of hopscotch to studying her a little too intently. 'Is that a loaded question?'

An important one. 'It stands to reason you might want your own family when you're so comfortable with this crowd.'

'You're right, I adore them. I fully intend on raising some kids of my own one day. What about you? You want a family some time?'

'Absolutely.' It was true. She did. People didn't always get everything they wanted, though. 'It's not something I've thought too much about lately.' Again true, because there'd never been a reason to. There hadn't been a man waiting in the wings to be a part of that life. Now there was a possibility of love happening she had to think how to go about this.

'Rosie and I had planned on starting a family as soon as I qualified.' His gaze had left her, appeared to have gone out across the lawn somewhere.

Molly touched his arm. 'Nathan? I'm sorry. I didn't mean to upset you.'

He looked at her, placing his hand over hers on his arm. 'You said sorry again.'

'Because I spoiled the moment.' He wanted a family. A bucket of cold water couldn't have chilled her any more than that information. It was the wake-up call she hated. Of course he'd want children when he fell in love again. It's what most men and women wanted. She did. Only it wasn't going to happen for her, and she wouldn't take anyone else on that ride. It would be grossly unfair to expect Nathan to drop his dream of children for her. A weight settled over her heart—the one that wasn't supposed to be involved with this amazing man.

'Get it into your head that talking about Rosie comes as naturally to me as eating. Sure, there're moments I feel sad, but it's a whole lot worse if she's never acknowledged.' He squeezed her hand, then let it go to step aside, putting space between them. 'If it's a problem for you then there's not a lot I can do. I will never deny she was the love of my life and how hard it's been to lose her.'

Collecting a few wake-up calls today. What was next? 'I like it that you feel that way. No one should be forgotten when they've been such a special part of your life. Hearing you talk about her says a lot about you, all good.' Her smile wavered, but since he wasn't watching her she got away with it. She wasn't going to be as special to him because even if he wanted that, she couldn't allow it to happen.

Instead she had to back off in case he did start to fall for her. That's when the day would come that she'd have to tell him the very long odds of her ever getting pregnant. Already she knew a quickening of her pulse whenever she heard Nathan's voice or laugh. Felt a softening of her limbs when he touched her. This had to stop. He'd been hurt once, she wasn't giving him a second blow.

'It helps you understand.' Nathan turned back to the barbecue. 'I'd better take over before the guys burn the steaks.' He hesitated, faced her again. 'We'll have some time to ourselves later.'

'I need to head home early. Catch up on sleep. And I'm working in the charity shop tomorrow.' She needed to think all this through. Unfortunately leaving now would be awkward after she'd helped set out the food and had said she couldn't wait to sample the salads.

'If that's what you want to do.' Nathan nodded abruptly. Sensing her withdrawal?

As soon as dinner was over and the kitchen cleaned up, she'd go home and revert to the Molly he used to know. No, not that. She'd be friendly and outgoing, but no more kisses. Already, walking away wouldn't be simple. Not when she'd finally come out of a drought to find she could be aroused by a man—one in particular.

But they weren't a couple. It was presumptuous to hope there might be more to Nathan's invitations and kisses than having a good time. It was quite possible he wanted to have some uncomplicated fun, and wasn't looking for a more permanent arrangement, and that she was reading too much into his friendliness. Something she'd be better thinking about than getting her knickers in a knot because he was the one helping her step back out into the real world.

Molly shoved aside all the reasons for not spending time with Nathan and said, 'It isn't, really. I don't know what came over me.' Except she did, and it wasn't going to disappear. She should leave, now. If only it was that easy. When she finally came out of her cave she didn't want to go back into the dark, cold space that her life had become.

'Gun-shy? I'm not surprised after meeting all this lot. It's enough to scare anyone off.'

'More that I feel very comfortable with them— too comfortable, maybe.'

He ruffled her hair like she'd seen him do with his nieces. 'Nothing wrong with comfortable.'

Yes, there was, if it led to greater expectations than were reasonable. But for tonight at least she'd relax and continue enjoying herself. And Nathan.

The family didn't leave early. It was as if they knew they were frustrating him. Nathan ground his teeth. Molly had said she'd leave after dinner, then changed her mind. Finally the brothers-in-law had made sounds about heading away and he'd had the front door open with embarrassing speed. But if they hadn't gone soon Molly might have, and he didn't want that. He wanted time with her not being interrupted by one of the children asking for more ice cream or a sister quizzing him on his next holiday plans.

'At last.' He shoved his hands in his pockets before he could haul Molly into his arms and kiss her senseless.

'You don't mean that.' She smiled as she stood in front of him, looking sensational with the riotous curls and that perfect body.

'Normally I'd agree, but tonight I just wanted to be with you for a while.' Hell, he wasn't going to be able to not kiss her.

Her breasts rose on an intake of air. 'I'm still here.'

'Tell me something I don't know.' He had to touch her. Had to. Placing his hands on her shoulders, he drew her closer. And closer. Until she was up against him, those breasts nudging his chest, her mouth so near to his. Then his mouth was on hers, kissing, tasting, drinking her in. As he kissed Molly he waited to see if she'd pull back or tense even a little, but, no, her arms were winding around his neck and her hips were pressing into his. Giving up on caution, he went deeper with the kiss, savouring Molly, her softness, her scent, all of her. Everything about her woke him up.

Then her mouth was gone. 'Nathan?' she gasped, blinking rapidly, no disappointment blazing out at him this time. But hope was, and enough desire to drown in.

'Yes, Mol. I'd like to take you to bed.'

She sank back against him, and returned to kissing the minutes away, until he couldn't take any more. Swinging her up into his arms, he asked, 'Bedroom?'

'No. Right here. Now.'

As he walked her up to the wall, he said, 'I'll be gentle.' No way did he want to frighten or hurt her.

'Don't you dare.' She lifted a leg to his thigh, freed her hands from his and wound them around his neck. 'I won't break.'

The corners of his mouth lifted. 'Tell me something I don't know.' Then he claimed her mouth, and placed his hands on her butt to lift her higher. When she wound her legs around him and settled against the growing evidence of his sex he had to take a deep breath and hold onto the need trying to break free. This wasn't just about him.

'Nathan,' she growled.

He returned to kissing, drawing out the exquisite moment for as long as possible. His mouth trailed below her ear, down her throat, to the neck of her jersey. 'Damn it. This has to go.'

How she did it he had no idea, but within moments her lace-covered breasts were before him, drying his mouth and tightening his groin to breaking point. Molly first. He pushed between them, slipped his hand under her trousers, then her underwear, and found her centre, and touched, caressed, and felt her blow apart with one hard, swift stroke.

She clung to him, hauling in gulps of air, her eyes barely open.

He waited, kissing her forehead, her breasts, her arm.

'Nathan, let me.' She wriggled in his hold, trying to unwind her legs from his torso.

'Steady,' he whispered against her feverish skin.

'Inside. I want you inside. It's your turn.'

'Shh. It's not about turns. I'm here, with you. We'll get together as soon as we remove the obstacle.' But, yes, he was more than ready.

She blinked. 'Obstacle?' Of course. 'Then let me down. I'll be quick.'

'You'd better be,' he grunted as he lowered her carefully and held her as she got rid of the rest of her clothes.

Then she was back in his arms, her legs wound around his waist. Lowering herself over his sex.

He couldn't halt the trembling throughout his body as he pushed deep inside. Molly held on tight as he withdrew and returned, winding her tighter and tighter until she exploded again. Then he let go, and rode the wave of desire, passion and need. Unbelievable.

Nathan stretched out in his bed, one hand behind his head, the other on Molly's breast as she slept. Earlier she'd been exhausted, and now after two bouts of lovemaking she'd succumbed, and had been comatose for a couple of hours.

Not that he minded. Lying here with her, listening to the soft snuffles she made, he couldn't have felt more relaxed or happy, in a way he hadn't expected to ever feel again. Though lately he'd been open to it, he just hadn't believed it might happen. Certainly not with Molly O'Keefe. Here was a woman who'd turned out to be nothing like the face she presented to the world. It could be that he hadn't known what to look for and her feisty, strong personality had been simmering in the background all along. Or it might be that with the divorce papers in her hands she'd found the hope and courage to go in search of the life she wanted.

Whatever it was, it didn't really matter, as long as he was a part of the future she unravelled. This had started as a challenge to make her like him, to be friendly towards him, but now the challenge had changed. He thought he might want her in his life—in all ways possible. Since Rosie no other woman had made him *want*. Love, a partner, family. Molly did that. *Rosie*. His heart slowed. He still missed her, but not as severely as in the past. Was he getting over the crippling loss? Did he want to have a future with another woman? Yeah, he thought he might. The only problem was that it was happening fast. Too fast?

'I'm glad your family turned up today or this might only be wishful thinking.' Molly's sleep-filled voice sounded sexy as hell.

As his body reacted in the only way it knew, he grinned, and caressed her breast, extracting a gasp of pleasure from her. 'You have an open invitation to visit any time you like.'

The sleep was rapidly disappearing from those sensational eyes, replaced with a sparkle that warmed his heart as Molly reached for him, wrapping her hand around his obvious attraction for her. 'Knock, knock, I'm here.'

'Can't argue with that,' he muttered as he leaned in to kiss that exquisite mouth, before exploring her body with his mouth. He couldn't get enough of her.

Hours later he woke suddenly as the bed rocked sharply.

'Look at the time.' Molly sounded frantic as

she tossed the covers aside, along with the arm he'd had around her waist. 'Ten past eight. I've got to be at the arena by nine.'

'There's plenty of time.'

'No, there's not. I can't be late, or Coach will send me packing permanently. I don't intend letting her down again.' She disappeared out the door, returned with last night's clothes, still yabbering. So unlike the Molly of the past. 'I have to get my gear from home and clothes to wear to the charity shop afterwards.'

Shoving the covers aside, Nathan stood up and stretched, and she didn't stop to notice. She was definitely on a mission. 'I'll put the coffee on. You want something to eat? Toast? Cereal?'

Finally she stopped and came to kiss him, a brief touch of those lips on his stubble-covered chin. Nowhere near enough. 'No, thanks. I'll grab something at home.' Then she was in the bathroom, the shower spraying out water and the extractor fan making a racket.

He knew when he was not needed. But if Molly thought he'd toe the line that easily, she was going to have to think again. In the bathroom he opened the shower door and joined her, taking the soap from her hands to wash her skin, starting at her neck, and working his way down to her feet. 'No complaints, madam?' He grinned through the water pouring over his head.

She waved a hand in the narrow space between them. 'How quick can you be?'

'Let me show you.'

When Molly dragged herself out of the shower not too much later and began drying her glistening skin, Nathan watched her while soaping himself. 'You're beautiful.'

Her head shot up, surprise widening her eyes.

He repeated himself. 'You are beautiful.'

Her hands hesitated in the process of towelling her stomach, and dropped to her thighs.

His gaze followed, then backed up to her lower belly. 'How'd you get that scar?' It was small, and stark against her pale skin.

The towel came up instantly, and the shutters came down over her eyes. 'I had an accident.' Then she was gone, out into his bedroom.

Snapping the shower off, Nathan picked up another towel and followed her. 'Molly, I'm sorry. I didn't mean anything by my question. I didn't even think before I asked.' The result of one of her ex's rages? Gritting his teeth, Nathan dried himself hard and fast.

Her face was blank. 'It's nothing, okay?'

No, it wasn't okay, but nothing would make him say so. His thoughtless question had already upset her. He was ready to murder someone.

Pausing in her rapid dressing, Molly looked

at him with sadness pouring off her in waves. 'Sorry to rush off like this.'

He suspected she was apologising for something entirely different. It took all his strength not to wrap her in his arms and tell her everything would be all right. Because he didn't know for sure that it would be, and making false promises was not the way to go. Instead he placed a hand on her cheek. 'Go impress Coach. I'll see you later, though probably not today.' He needed some space while he thought through everything that had been happening between them.

Molly didn't look unhappy with that. 'It's fine. I've got stuff to do after basketball.' She was already making her way to the door, where she paused and looked directly at him. 'I had the best night.'

Steal his breath, why didn't she? 'So did I, Molly. So did I.' It was true. So true it was scary. And exciting. And something to think about.

CHAPTER NINE

'HI, VICKI. I'M not going to ask how your weekend went. It's written all over your face.' Vicki had headed north to Darwin to spend time with Cole when he wasn't on duty.

Molly banged her locker shut and pocketed her key. When Vicki didn't reply she looked closer. 'Oh, hell. Come here.' Regretting her comment, she reached to hug her friend.

Palms out towards her, Vicki shook her head. 'Don't. I'll fall apart if you're kind to me.'

'Fair enough.' How awful to have her husband heading away so soon for who knew how long. Molly went for a complete change of subject. 'I see you've gone all out today. Love that shade of purple in your top, and as for the boots, I'm drooling.' Relief glittered out of Vicki's sad eyes. 'Took me weeks to find boots to match my outfit. Finally found them in a second-hand shop. This is not my usual style of clothes. I'm more the black on black type. Except for the shoes.'

'Except for the shoes,' Molly said at the same time, and they burst out laughing. Leaning back against her locker, she waited while Vicki changed into her uniform. 'Hope we have a quiet night.'

'I want it so busy I don't come up for air.'

'One of us should get lucky, then.' Her ears were straining for the sound of Nathan's voice out in the department. She hadn't seen him when she'd arrived, and as he was always early he had to be tied up with a patient already.

'You been for a spin in Nathan's fancy car yet?'

'I was too busy.' Doing other things with Nathan, and avoiding certain issues that weren't going to go away no matter how much she wanted them to.

'Doing what?' Disappointment blinked out at her.

Vicki wanted her to get with Nathan? Then she'd be pleased to know what had gone on between them, but Molly wasn't spilling the beans. She didn't do juicy gossip, and when it involved herself she remained especially tight-lipped. She straightened up. 'Better get cracking and start earning my living.' Away from the questions that were likely with Vicki needing a distraction from her aching heart.

'I'll be right there.'

Joining the rest of the shift waiting for change-over, Molly still couldn't see or hear Nathan. She should be relieved, not sad. Having decided to go for friendly and easy with him, disappointed wasn't an option. Saturday night had been sensational. Not a lot of sleep, though. Instead she'd had quite a workout, and still wanted more.

'Morning, everyone. Hope you had a good weekend.' Nathan strode in with a large smile and sparkling eyes as he scanned the room, pausing for a moment when he saw her. The smile brightened briefly, then he seemed to remember where he was, who he was with, and he straightened. 'Right, let's get the show on the road.' He came to stand beside Molly, though.

Her body was doing the happy dance on the inside while externally she tried to keep her face still while listening to Mick run through the patients in the department. It wasn't easy when she was fighting the desire to curl into Nathan, struggling with the need to touch him, to feel his warm skin under her palms.

'Cubicle one, forty-two-year-old male, waiting for liver function tests to be completed. In two, fifty-six-year-old female, extreme abdo pain, query diverticulosis.' Mick continued through the list of patients, and Molly felt tired before they'd started.

'You okay?' Nathan asked quietly as everyone dispersed to get on with the shift.

Why was he asking? 'I'm good. Did you get the place cleaned up yesterday?'

'Eventually.' His smile was devastating.

'You went back to sleep.' She grinned.

'Quiet, woman, unless you want everyone knowing why I was so exhausted.' His whispered words sent a thrill of excitement down her spine.

How was she going to remain focused on not getting too close to this man who'd woken her up from her dull and cautious life?

Mick was talking to the triage nurse and now turned to Molly. 'Can you take this one? Twenty-one-year-old male, stab wounds to his face and arms. I'll send someone else to help you in a mo.'

'On my way.' She checked which cubicle to use, glad of something to keep her busy and away from Nathan, because even standing beside him made her weak at the knees.

Got it bad, Mol?

Yeah, she was beginning to think so.

'I'll check the man out with Molly, Mick. Those stab wounds might need my sewing skills.'

So much for putting space between them. But what could she say? She liked working with him, even when they hadn't been comfortable together. He was a superb emergency specialist, and she learnt from watching him. So she went to meet her patient and settle him on the bed in cubicle eleven as the triage nurse gave them the details.

'Beau Cooper, twenty-one, stabbed with a broken bottle, significant wound to his face, minor cuts on both arms.' Sally turned to the young woman who'd accompanied him. 'Gina, here, is Beau's girlfriend. She brought him in.'

'Hi, Beau. I'm Molly, one of the nurses who's going to look after you.' She turned to Nathan. 'This is Dr Lupton.'

Nathan moved up to examine the young man's face. 'Beau, tell me what happened when you were attacked. Did you fall to the ground, bang your head? Any details are important.'

'I'm not sure. Two guys attacked me when I asked for my girlfriend's bag back. They smashed a beer bottle and got me in the head, the arms and my leg. I stayed upright, didn't hit my head on anything. That's all I can tell you.'

'How's your breathing? Are you having any difficulty with that?'

'Seems all right.'

Then the glass hadn't cut through anything vital in his throat. Holding her hand up, Molly moved it from left to right. 'Follow my hand.'

Beau's eyes slid sideways, focused on her movements.

'Good, your vision checks out.'

The curtains flicked wide and Hank joined them. 'Nathan, you're wanted in three urgently.'

'On my way.' Nathan turned to her. 'I'll be back when you've cleaned him up.'

After a quick rundown on what had happened, Hank said, 'I'll remove his jeans so we can check his legs for abrasions.'

Molly nodded. 'Might as well. Though from the small amount of blood I don't think there's anything too serious in that region, but he needs to get out of the messy clothes anyway.' The wound in Beau's neck and face was deep, his neck had damaged muscles that would require surgery that couldn't happen until the morning. She began swabbing the area, careful not to cause him any more distress.

Hank got Beau to lift his hips while he tugged the jeans off.

Their patient groaned but did as asked.

'I'll get you some penicillin next,' Hank told him. 'Who knows what was on that bottle?'

'Get something to numb the pain too.' Molly had finished cleaning the man's neck and face, and dropped the swabs into a hazardous waste bin at the head of the bed. 'I'm going to talk to Dr Lupton, Beau.'

Nathan was entering notes on a patient file on the screen. 'How's your man?'

'I'll be interested to hear what you say after you take a look at the neck and face wound. I think he needs surgery.'

Nathan's chair rolled back from the desk and those long legs pushed him upward. 'Any other serious injuries?'

'Not really. Hank's getting some drugs. The guy's in a lot of pain and trying not to show it.'

'The tough type.'

'That's because he's a boxer,' Beau's girlfriend told them minutes later. 'They're expected to take the knocks without complaining.'

'Why did those men have your handbag?' Molly asked Gina as she handed Hank the pain-killer drug and checked the dates with him.

'Thought they were being clever,' Beau snarled. 'They reckoned they were better than me and could help themselves to my girlfriend.'

'Don't let them get to you. You'll only upset yourself and I'd prefer you stay calm and get on with recovering.' Nathan was at the side of the bed. 'I need to look at your wound. That all right with you?'

'Yeah.' Beau nodded, then grimaced and swore.

'Tip your head sideways. That's it.'

After a thorough examination Nathan told his

patient, 'You're lucky. There's no serious damage, but a plastic surgeon will have to put it back together so you're not left with an ugly scar. In the meantime I'll put in a few temporary stitches to keep the wound closed, and the bleeding to a minimum.'

'Thanks,' Beau muttered, reaching out for his girlfriend's hand, looking scared.

'You'll be fine,' Molly said. 'I'll get the gear.'

Nathan told his patient, 'This means you'll stay in overnight.'

When Molly returned, Nathan was scrubbing his hands at the sink before pulling on gloves. She placed the suture kit on the small table next to him.

Behind her Gina was saying, 'I'll phone your mum, tell her what's happened.' Out of the corner of her eye Molly saw the girlfriend tighten her grip on Beau's hand. 'Love you,' she added as his face screwed up.

'Don't call the olds.'

'They need to know where you are. What if the police ring them?'

'I suppose.'

'Right.' Nathan stepped up to the bed. 'Let's get this out of the way.'

Molly saw Gina's face whiten. 'Why don't you go out to the waiting room to make that call? You can come back any time you like, just tell them who you're with and they'll open the security door.'

'Thanks.' Gina's relief was obvious in her speed to get away before Nathan started stitching the wound.

'Have you spoken to the police yet?' Nathan asked Beau in an attempt to distract him from the tugging and snipping as he placed stitches along the edges of the wound.

'Gina did. They're going to press charges, so I suppose they'll turn up here.'

As soon as Nathan had finished, Molly went to tell Gina it was all right to come back, and then she went to see a ninety-three-year-old who'd been found wandering in the rain in the gardens of the rest home where she lived. 'How are you feeling, Mrs Grooby?'

The old lady opened her eyes and focused on Molly. Nothing wrong there. 'I'm good.'

'What about the last couple of days? Everything all right?' She was gaunt and looked very pale. According to the rest-home staff she'd become quite vague lately, yet right now she was alert and beginning to watch everything going on out in the department.

'I think so.'

The notes said Mrs Grooby had been disorientated when she'd arrived two hours ago. A medical event, or lonely and seeking attention?

'I'm going to ask you silly questions. Can you answer them for me?'

'Yes, dear.'

'What's our national animal?'

'A kangaroo.'

'What do people get from a library?'

'Books, of course.'

'Count backwards from ten for me.'

As the old lady muttered numbers in the correct order, Molly tidied up her bed cover and watched her patient. 'No problem. You slayed the test.'

'I heard all that. Nothing wrong with your mind, Mrs Grooby,' Nathan announced as he strolled into the cubicle.

Was he following her around? He couldn't be. Since it was a quiet night he could be trying to keep busy too. 'She's lonely,' Molly said quietly as she passed him.

He nodded. 'We see that often with the oldies.'

'You two talking about me?' Mrs Grooby's eyes lit up.

Molly chuckled. 'You're too sharp for your own good. Would you like a cup of tea?'

'Yes, please. And a biscuit?'

'Of course.' Molly headed down to the kitchen and sneaked a biscuit for herself while she waited for the tea bag to brew. Only an hour in and already she was hungry. It had to be a result of running around the basketball court Saturday and Sunday.

Mick stuck his head in the door. 'There are two ambulances on the way in with an elderly couple who were in a multiple car pile-up. Nothing serious, mostly cuts and bruises, and shock. You and Hank take them when they get here.'

'Onto it.'

The couple was shaken but alert as they were wheeled into adjacent cubicles and transferred from the stretchers to beds. The curtain between was pulled back and when Mrs Andrews tried to reach her husband's hand, Hank and Molly moved the beds closer. 'There you go.'

'Some date this turned out to be,' Colin Andrews winked at his wife. 'Should've stayed home and watched the tele.'

'I don't know. It's quite exciting in here,' his wife returned.

'Where were you off to?' There was a storm raging over the city, and it was bitterly cold out. Molly had worn her puffer jacket into work.

'It's our fifty-third wedding anniversary, and we always visit the church we were married in on the day. We didn't have time earlier what with all the family dropping in and out like we run the best diner in town.'

Mrs Andrews's gruff voice made Molly glance at her. Something wasn't sitting right.

'Has anyone got in touch with a member of your family?' Molly asked as she sponged the lady's arms where small cuts from windscreen glass had caused bleeding.

'You don't want them descending on the ED,' Colin answered quickly. 'Too noisy.'

'You can't tell one without telling them all,' his wife hastened to add.

When Molly lifted her patient's arm she felt a tremor in the soft muscles. There was definitely something not quite right going on.

'We'll sort it,' Colin growled.

Glancing at Hank, Molly saw he'd also got the sense something was wrong. But what could they do? Their role was to patch people up and send them home again, or pass them on to specialists and wards, not to solve family problems. 'Right, I'm going to do a bit of stitching.'

'Bet you're not as good at it as Sylvia. She used to make wedding dresses for the nobs.'

'Is that so? Then she can sew you back together when I've finished with her.' Molly laughed. 'Can I get you both a cup of tea while I'm at it?'

'Best offer I've had all night.' Colin smiled, relief underlining his words. So getting in touch with their family was a no-no.

As it wasn't her place to interfere, Molly let it go with a heavy heart. Families were so important, and to lose one was beyond comprehension. When her mother had insisted she was wrong about Paul, that he'd never meant to hurt her, she'd felt she'd lost everything—her marriage *and* her family. Nowadays her mother was working hard at getting back onside, and as much as Molly wanted that, she was taking a cautious approach. 'Tea along with the needles and thread coming up.'

'Molly.' Mike appeared round the corner of the hub. 'Sixteen-year-old girl, overdosed on paracetamol. Resus, please. Hank, you okay in here?'

'Sure.'

'On my way.' Shuddering, she sped along to the well-equipped room and straight up to the bed where Nathan, a junior doctor and another nurse were working with the teen while an ambulance paramedic was filling them in on the scant details.

'The mother thinks she swallowed at least twenty tablets. When they found her she was unconscious, but has since woken and been throwing up.'

'Resultant liver damage will be the biggest concern,' Nathan explained to the other doctor as he listened to the medic reading out the obs she'd taken on the ride in. 'If she's been vomiting then I don't think it's necessary to pump the stomach. I'll give her some charcoal to soak up any remaining traces of drugs in her digestive system.'

Molly began wiping the girl to clean her up. Along with the other nurse, they stripped her and dressed her in a gown and got rid of the grubby clothes.

'Nathan, you're needed next door,' someone called.

'Now we're getting busy.' He looked to Molly, a wry smile lifting his mouth. 'That'll keep us on our toes and too busy for anything else.'

'Seems like it.' She smiled back. Why did he have to be so sexy even when dressed in a boring green uniform? This should be the one time her mind didn't drag up images of him looking like a centrefold, or holding her against his naked body, or sitting opposite her having breakfast in the café.

When he joined her and Hank in the café for coffee and sandwiches just after eight, she was glad they weren't alone or she might've dropped her intention of keeping him at a distance—a very short one—while at work. He was near irresistible.

'You survived my lot okay.' Nathan bit into a

thick bread roll filled with meat and a dash of salad. 'They can be intimidating.'

'I enjoyed myself, so thanks for inviting me along.'

Hank's eyebrows rose, before he went back to checking his phone for messages.

'You obviously like kids,' Nathan observed.

Hadn't they done this on Saturday? Because of her scar had he guessed there might be an issue with her infertility? 'Who doesn't?'

I'm not seeing where this is going.

'Not everyone thinks children are the best thing since sliced bread.'

'Certainly everyone in your family does. I'm only surprised you're capable of walking without a limp. They used you as a trampoline half the time.'

'I'm used to it. Though as they get bigger I'm going to have to tone down the level of bounce.' He was watching her like there was no one else in the room, and certainly had no qualms about Hank knowing they'd spent time together.

Hank put his phone down and picked up his mug. 'I've seen Nathan bruised and limping after a round of ball games with the Lupton bunch. He hurt for days, and got no sympathy from any of us.'

Nathan grinned. 'You were pathetic, not joining in to help me out.'

'A group of us were at Nathan's for a barbecue when some of his family showed up unexpectedly. Those kids took over like they owned the place, and we had a lot of laughs watching Uncle Nathan do his impersonation of an active seven-year-old for hours on end.'

'I know what you mean.' Obviously she wasn't the first he'd invited to his house. Why did she think she might've been when they were having a party there next weekend? It was his way of being friendly, and she'd thought there was more to it. Though he'd offered her the flat to live in. After kissing her. And now he'd made love to her. 'Kind of cute, I think.' She grinned at Nathan, who screwed his face up. 'Shows he's not always the boss.'

'I'm getting another coffee. You two need any?' Hank stood up.

'No, thanks,' Molly and Nathan answered simultaneously.

She watched Hank walk across the room, stopping to yarn with nurses from the general ward.

'I missed you yesterday.'

Knock me over with a feather.

'You did?' Warmth stole through her, softening all those knots that had begun tightening since she'd seen how much he adored his nieces and nephews and heard how he wanted to add to the bunch.

'Yes. I came that close…' he held up two fingers only millimetres apart '…to driving over to your apartment late yesterday but I know you were busy at the charity shop.' His smile hit her in the chest. 'Anyway, I sat down on the couch, and didn't know a thing until seven.'

'You old man, you.'

'You think?'

'Not for a minute.' This was fun, and relaxing, and she could do it for ever. Except—

Shut up, conscience. Let me have some fun before it's time to get real.

'Sorry I had to race away but that's how it is.' Now that she was getting a life.

'It wouldn't be if you moved into the flat.'

She hadn't seen that coming. Leaning back in the hard plastic chair, she tried to lift the blinkers and study Nathan as others might see him. There was much to like, to trust, to love even. And she couldn't help the way he turned her on, how she wanted to be with him more often. But, 'Everything's happening in a hurry. I need to keep my own space at the moment.'

'Fair enough.' His face lost its relaxed expression. 'I understand. But I'm an impatient brute at times.'

'The last thing you are is a brute, Nathan. Believe me, I know.'

He gulped, and sighed. 'It was a loose term. I need to learn to be careful of my words around you.'

She shook her head. 'No, you don't. I need to lighten up. Though I thought I was doing okay.'

'You know what? We've suddenly become serious. This isn't the place to be mentioning what's happened to you so let's relax again.' There was a plea in his eyes.

She nodded, more than happy to go along with him. 'Done.'

'So how many awkward questions did the sisters ask you?'

'Not one.' She'd been as surprised as Nathan looked. 'Not usual?'

'Not at all. My sisters believe there're no rules when it comes to their brother.' He drained his coffee.

'Families know all the buttons to push.' Would Gran have liked Nathan? She had no idea why but Molly thought she probably would have, and that gave her comfort.

'I'm glad you had a good time and enjoyed being with the kids.'

'Nathan...' She swallowed. Every time he mentioned the kids and her in the same sentence the worry intensified. It was beginning to seem like she wouldn't be able to have a few weeks of fun before telling him the truth. To be fair, that would be selfish of her. Sometime in the next few days they were going to have a full and frank conversation about her fertility—or lack of.

'Hey, guys, we're needed. All hands on deck. A van full of American tourists rolled on the highway and the first ones are expected here in ten.' Mick was already moving away in search of more ED staff.

'Mondays are supposed to be quiet,' Nathan muttered before he took a last mouthful of his roll.

CHAPTER TEN

WHAT WAS MOLLY'S PROBLEM? She seemed all out of sync. One moment happy beyond description, the next eyeing him with trepidation. Nathan watched her calming a teenager whose friends had brought her in with numerous bee stings.

'You're not having a reaction.' Molly wiped the girl's arms. 'Yes, you copped a lot of stings, which have been removed, and you're hurting, but your windpipe is not about to close up.'

He stepped in. 'Hi, I'm Nathan, a doctor. What Molly's telling you is correct. If you'd had an allergic reaction your throat, tongue and face would be swelling by now.' He hoped that backing Molly and playing it down would quieten the shrieking, shaking girl. 'Just to make absolutely certain, let me have a look inside your mouth.'

Instant quiet returned to the area as Becky's mouth fell open for him. After his examination, he told her, 'Looking healthy. Now let me touch your neck and throat.' With gentle fingers he felt for any sign of swelling. 'Again, all good.'

Molly smiled at her, and *his* gut twisted. He had it bad. The week since his family had been in town had been sensational. Lots of laughter, shared meals and unbelievable sex. There'd been tender moments too, like when she'd made his favourite breakfast and set it out on the conservatory table with a flower in one of his beer glasses because he didn't own a vase. He did now. Molly had found him the ugliest pottery creation imaginable at the charity shop. The vase had pride of place in a hidden corner of his office. Molly had threatened to buy flowers and bring the hideous thing out for tomorrow night's party with the medical team. Who would have believed she could be such a tease? Especially with him. It was great.

'Becky, you'll soon get very itchy to go with the pain and swelling.' Molly nudged him none too gently with her elbow. 'Dr Lupton will give you something to relieve that as much as possible.'

'I'll prescribe a cream to save you having to buy one. Just apply it a couple of times until the itching stops.' Nathan nodded as he mentally ran through the available remedies, all the while trying not to laugh out loud at Molly's temerity for giving him the get-a-grip look in here. But she was right. He shouldn't get distracted by her while at work. Though how not to he had no idea. It would be better to start by staying away from patients she was involved with.

'So I'm not going to have anaphylactic shock?' Becky sounded disappointed.

'No, I'm pleased to say you're not.' Did she want attention that badly she'd risk her life? 'Have you ever seen anyone suffer one?'

'A boy at school had one once. Everyone was around him like you wouldn't believe, and he got taken away in the ambulance. He nearly died. Heaps of kids went to see him in hospital afterwards.'

Uh-huh. 'I think there are better ways of getting people to take notice of you. Like being the person who organises the others to go visiting someone who's sick. Being the sick person sucks. Apart from the pain and all the things medical staff do to you, it's boring lying around in bed all day. Especially in hospital where it's noisy and the nurses come and poke at your body any time they like.'

Molly had turned away, her sexy mouth twitching nonstop.

Becky was eyeing him warily. 'What's the food like?'

It was hard not to laugh, even though this was

one mixed-up girl. 'Nothing fancy, but it passes. But you won't be finding out. You can go home shortly.' He turned away before Becky could come up with some symptom that might let her stay in overnight. 'Molly, can you get the cream for Becky when I've signed the form?'

'Sure.' She turned to their patient. 'Want your girlfriends to come in now?'

'They won't be waiting for me.'

Molly stepped closer to the bed. 'They were still there fifteen minutes ago. The triage nurse told me.'

'Really? Can they really come in?'

'I'll get them right now.' Molly headed away.

Nathan went to write up the notes on Becky. Twenty-thirty. Half an hour before he could think about heading home or to Molly's apartment. Not too long, if all went according to plan.

'Nathan.' Mick appeared in front of him. 'You're needed in Resus. Unconscious thirty-one-year-old male, fell from the third floor of an apartment, severe head injuries, punctured left lung, fractured femur both legs, and that's only the obvious.'

He moved fast, heading for Resus right on Mick's heels. So much for plans. But if he had to be waylaid then this was what he wanted to be doing more than anything.

Except it wasn't.

They worked their butts off trying to save Mason Haverstock, every staff member in Resus giving their best and more. To no avail. Mason's heart gave out due to blood loss and trauma from fractured ribs.

Nathan went into withdrawal, automatically closing everything down and signing off the case. Only when he talked to the man's wife and parents did he drag himself out of the funk the death had brought on—because he understood the pain he was inflicting by telling the crying woman what had happened. His words were intractable, and were stealing her dreams, her love, her future. These moments had always been hard, but for him they'd become almost personal since Rosie's death.

Next he went for a brisk walk around town, barely noticing the drizzle and cool breeze. What was a bit of weather when your heart was breaking?

Nearly two hours later he texted Molly from outside her apartment block. You awake? There was light behind the blinds of her bedroom so he wasn't waking her. He hoped. Anyway, if she was asleep she wouldn't hear the text land in her phone. He'd given up on the walk, had headed for home, and instead ended up here.

Molly would know what he wanted. She also understood pain.

Come up. The door into the building clicked open.

'I need a hug,' Nathan said the moment he reached the third floor and found her standing in her doorway, dressed in a thick white robe.

Molly nudged the door shut with her hip and reached for him, wrapped her arms around his waist and pulled him close to nestle her face against his neck. 'That bad?'

'That bad.' He nodded against her. The guy had only been thirty-one, for Pete's sake. All his life ahead of him. A wife and two little girls left behind. Life was a bitch at times. A real ugly bitch. Nathan's arms tightened around Molly's warmth, and he absorbed her strength, the understanding, like a man starved.

Time disappeared as they stood there, Molly's soft hands beneath his shirt, caressing his back, slowly, tenderly. All he knew was that this was where he had to be, who he had to be with while the darkness roiled, then began to fade.

Finally Molly lifted her head enough to look at him. 'Tea? Or something stronger?'

He knew too well from the past that something stronger wouldn't fix his pain over losing a patient. It might blank out things if he drank enough, but those sights would return when he woke up with a mighty hangover and nothing solved. Then he'd feel a failure for being weak. 'Tea. Lots of it.'

Her smile was filled with understanding and care. Love? No, it couldn't be. Not this soon. That had to be wishful thinking. He wanted Molly to love him? Possibly. They had been having an amazing time, and he couldn't see it slowing down any time soon. But was that love? Or was he reacting to the aftermath of a gruelling night in the ED? Her smile had gone right to the tips of his toes, filling every space in his body, and his mind. His arms tightened around her again. 'In a minute.'

They drank tea, Molly's legs curled under her curvy butt on the small couch, while Nathan half lay in one of the chairs, stretching his legs across the room, his mug held in both hands as he talked out the gremlins. She asked no questions, made no comments about what he'd done for his patient, just listened, and accepted, and understood.

He hadn't had that before. Not even from Rosie. She'd hated hearing anything about his work except when they'd saved someone and even then she'd only wanted the bare, happy facts. It was the only area of his life she hadn't understood as much as he'd wanted. Yet here

Molly was, totally getting his mood. As a nurse, she knew what it was like to face hell in the department.

They went to bed, holding each other like they'd never let go. Then in the early hours they made love, slowly, tenderly, and filled with so much care and—and love. Afterwards Nathan lay on his back, his hand on Molly's butt as she lay sprawled on her stomach, sound asleep, and he stared upwards into the dark.

Love. Was that what this was? This sense of coming home, of belonging to another person in a way not even his family could give him? Love. Yes, that's what these feelings and sensations were about. Love. That softening in his belly whenever he touched Molly, listened to her sharp voice and her light laughter, smelled her scent, saw that lithe body move sometimes as though on hot coals and at others as though she was dancing through the air.

It had happened in a flash, their relationship doing a one-eighty in weeks. Who'd have believed it could happen to him again? Not again. This was different. With Rosie they'd always been in each other's lives, had grown up falling in love. With Molly, a snap of his fingers and, *voilà*, he was a goner.

Rolling onto his side, Nathan scooped Molly against the length of his body and closed his eyes.

* * *

Molly woke instantly. No slow stretching, opening her eyes one at a time. Just ping. It was Saturday morning and tonight was the work barbecue.

Nathan held her against him as though he never wanted to let her go. Soft snores told her he was out to it. Good. He needed to move on from last night's tragedy. Not that it would vanish from his mind easily. They never did. The downside to working in medicine was the toll it could take. Snuggling harder against him, she thought about last night's lovemaking. It had been very different from the other times. Slow, and caring. She'd given everything in her to Nathan, hoping to ease his pain. It must've worked, judging by his comatose state. He'd never before slept beyond sunrise with her.

Reaching for her phone, she sat up in a hurry when '08.05' blinked at her. There was a dessert to make and get into the freezer before she got ready for basketball, and then she'd promised to go round to Nathan's house straight after to help with anything he hadn't got done.

'Morning,' came a sleepy voice beside her. Then an arm began pulling her back under the covers.

'Oh, no, you don't. We've got things to do.' She pushed away.

Nathan tugged her again, causing her to sprawl across his frame. 'Starting with this.'

She gave in. How could she not?

It was the perfect way to start the day. Followed by Nathan poaching eggs and frying bacon while she made a lemon dessert. When she felt his gaze on her, she turned from whipping the cream cheese. 'What?'

'You're singing. I like it.'

'I was?' Definitely getting back to normal.

Next she hit the court with the Roos, and they stole the game fifty-eight to thirty-five.

Bypassing the after-match celebrations again, Molly headed home for a shower and to get dressed in red and white for the evening. Then she drove to Nathan's and found Vicki already there, running around with a vacuum cleaner and duster.

'I don't know why she's bothering. By the time everyone leaves tonight the place will be a lot messier than it is now.' Nathan scratched his head.

'She needs the distraction,' Molly muttered. Vicki had been valiantly trying to be cheerful all week since returning from Darwin, but everyone saw through her attempts. 'It must be hard, saying goodbye to her man so often.' She'd hate that, couldn't imagine being married to someone who was often away for long stints.

'It gets to Cole too,' Nathan admitted. 'I don't know why he went and signed up in the first place. I get wanting to do something for your country, but it's hard on family and friends, and yourself. I doubt I could do it. In a way I admire him.'

Molly's sympathy lay with Vicki, but she kept that to herself. Holding up the plastic container she'd brought, she said, 'I'll put this in the freezer and find something useful to do.'

'I hate to tell you this but everything's pretty much ready. We can kick back and relax once madam's finished making a racket with the sucky motor machine.'

'You've been spending too much time with your nephews. Sucky motor. I'll give you sucky.'

'I wish, but we're not alone.'

Molly headed for the kitchen, swallowing her laughter. Nathan was so relaxed it was hard to believe he was the same man she'd known only a couple of weeks ago.

'You two have come a long way in a short time,' Vicki said with a grin minutes later as she packed the cleaner into its cupboard.

She couldn't have overheard their banter. 'True. We're not about to kill each other any more.'

'It's great. He needs someone like you in his life. Make that he needs *you*.'

Molly looked around for Nathan. Having him overhear Vicki was the last thing she wanted.

'Relax. He's out in the conservatory, making sure there's enough gas for the barbecue. It should've been the first thing he checked. But that's Nathan.'

'What do you mean by that?'

'He can be the most disorganised male you've ever met when he's not at work. It used to drive Cole bonkers when they were flatting together.' Vicki headed for the kitchen. 'Ready for a drink? I'm not talking coffee or tea.'

'Why not? Everyone will be turning up soon.' As long as Vicki didn't start going on about Nathan she was happy to relax. Relax. A new word in her vocabulary. Suddenly relaxing had become part of her routine, along with having fun and mixing with people without looking over her shoulder. And starting to trust a man. 'I'll have a beer.'

'Coming up.'

She sank down onto the cane couch in the little nook off the kitchen where she could see out across the lawn to the sea, and if she turned her head slightly to the left Nathan out in the conservatory filled her sight, rubbing the stainless-steel lid of the state-of-the-art barbecue, bringing out the shine.

'Here.'

She took the bottle and settled down further into the thick cushions. 'This is the life.' Then she sat up straight. That might sound like she was trying to weave her way into Nathan's home for her own gain. 'I mean, how better to spend a Saturday afternoon than with friends?'

'Take it easy. You're more than a friend to Nathan.' Vicki was eyeing her over the top of her own bottle. 'I meant what I said before. You're good for him, and I think he's good for you. I don't know anything about your life before you came to work with us, but you've changed since my birthday. I'm putting some of that down to Nathan. Am I right?'

This was what good friends did. They talked, and then she'd have to give some answers back. She wasn't ready for that. Or was she? 'Yes, you're right.' Looking outside again, she sighed with happiness. Then an image of Nathan chasing his nephews across the lawn out there swiped her, and the warmth that had started filling her slowed, chilled. Children. He'd made no bones about wanting a family. He'd been honest, whereas she'd lied—if only by omission.

'Molly? What's wrong?'

Her gaze drifted back to the man tipping her world upside down. She wanted to tell Vicki nothing was wrong, but she couldn't. 'It's early days. We don't know each other very well yet.'

She knew he liked having his inner thighs stroked, that it hurt deeply when he lost a patient, that he adored his nieces and nephews. Family. She stood up. 'Let's see what else needs doing.'

'Molly, sit down, and I promise to shut up.'

Because she wanted friends in her life and not just as numbers on her phone, she plonked her backside back on the couch. Anyway, she liked Vicki and didn't want to upset her. 'Here's to a great night.'

'I'm going to put some music on. I never could understand why Nathan doesn't have it playing all the time.'

'Because I like to hear myself think.' The man himself lounged against the central kitchen bench, a beer between his fingers and a lopsided smile on his face.

Molly sucked in her stomach. It was so unfair. He was gorgeous. He was everything she wanted in a man when she moved forward.

Hey, you are moving forward.

Yes, but there was some way to go before she'd allow permanence into the picture. Even though things were beginning to stack up as she wanted, it was early days.

While the other two gave each other cheek and talked about people and events she knew nothing about, Molly did some serious thinking. She had begun falling for Nathan too quickly.

She trusted him as she'd once trusted Paul. He was fun, and caring, and sharing. Paul had once been fun, and caring, but sharing had been replaced by selfishness. She needed to step back, get to know Nathan better, if he hung around—and he acted as though he intended to.

Which brought her to the real problem. She had to tell him the truth. Because if she did fall in love with him, that was far too late.

'You going to daydream all afternoon?' Nathan tapped her shoulder.

If only that's what she was doing. Forcing a smile, she said, 'Got any better suggestions?'

He laughed, which went some way to lightening her mood again. But the clock was ticking. She had to tell him she couldn't have children.

'I didn't think they'd ever leave.' Nathan locked the door behind Hank and Myra before trailing into the kitchen where Molly was putting the last of the dirty glasses in the dishwasher.

'They've really gone?' Her knuckles were white as she gripped a dirty beer mug. She'd become more distant as the night had progressed.

What's up, Mol?

'The place is quiet, isn't it? Apart from the music, and I've lowered the decibels considerably. I might have to drop leftover desserts in to the neighbours in the morning as an apology.'

'Good luck with that. I don't think there's much left.' Glasses rattled against the wire rack as she put the mug in the washer.

'Want a nightcap?' They could sit and talk in the nook, where it was warm and cosy.

'No, thanks.'

'Tea?'

'No.'

'Bed?'

Shaking her head, she shut the washer and flicked the dials. Then she leaned back against the bench, her hands gripping the edge of the counter at her sides. Apart from the low hum of water swirling inside the dishwasher the house was quiet. Too quiet. Filling with foreboding.

Nathan rushed to fill the eerie silence before Molly could ruin the warm fuzzy feeling he got when he was with her. 'Thanks for all you did tonight.' She'd been a trouper, setting out food, clearing up after everyone, making sure no one went without a drink while barely touching one herself. 'You were taught how to be the hostess with the mostest?'

Her chin jerked down once. 'Yes. Part of being my mother's daughter was the social training that went on every day, no matter what else was happening.'

Had Molly ever been herself, doing what she wanted, how she wanted? Or had the basketball, the nursing degree and whatever other things she'd achieved been done because she'd been put under pressure? Had she spent all her life trying to please others? He wouldn't expect that of her. Ever. 'Now you can do whatever you want. You could even have tipped Carry's drink over his face when he started making rude suggestions to you and Myra.'

'I came close, believe me.' She shrugged. 'It's all right. He'd had too much to drink and will probably fall over backwards apologising on Monday.'

'True. It's not the first time, and won't be the last. I'd like to not invite him to these dos, but he's one of the team, one of the best, and everyone has their issues.'

So what's yours tonight, Molly?

'He'll pay you back for the taxi you organised. You're right, he is one of the best—when he's sober.' Worry was in her gaze, making her nibble her lip and turning those knuckles whiter than ever.

'Talk to me.'

Her eyebrows lifted, fell back into place. 'Too clever for your own good, you are.'

The foreboding increased. This was about him. He'd swear on his next breakfast Molly was about to dump on him. Or walk away for ever. His gut tightened as nausea rose. They weren't an item so how could she drop him? This called for something stronger than a beer that had gone flat over the hour since he'd opened the bottle. Standing, he reached around Molly for the wine bottle.

She flinched.

Slowly withdrawing his hand without touching the bottle, he backed off two steps. 'I'd never hurt you,' he ground out through clenched jaws. 'Never.' It hurt for her to think differently.

'I know.'

'So what was that about?' They'd come far, or so he'd thought. Guess it wasn't easy to get over what had been done to her.

'I'm sorry.'

He hated that word coming from Molly. It came loaded with the need to please, to be safe, and she did not have to do that around him. 'You don't owe me an apology for anything. But I would like an explanation.'

Her breath intake was ragged. 'You're right. You're owed one.' She was being too compliant.

He wanted to shake her gently, make her stop being that person and return to being the Molly he was getting to know, but instead he poured a small wine and returned to sit down, giving her space, wishing he could wrap her in a big hug and hold her until she never, ever felt afraid again. He should be able to without worrying he was making her uncomfortable. 'I thought we were getting close enough to talk about most things.'

Especially since you told me about your ex.

'I think I will have a drink after all.'

He started to get up to get it for her but she put up a hand in the stop signal.

When she sloshed as much wine on the bench as into her glass Nathan knew he was in trouble.

Putting his drink aside, he sat straighter, needing to focus on Molly and whatever was worrying her. He waited. His gut churned. His heart thumped hard and heavy. And he waited.

Perching on a stool, she sipped her drink and put the glass aside to jam her shaking hands between her knees. Then finally she raised her head and eyeballed him.

He wished she hadn't. He would far prefer her not to say a word, to carry on with the silent treatment. There was something in her look that said his world as it had become was about to disintegrate. Rushing in, he said, 'You can trust me not to hurt you that way.'

You're repeating yourself.

'Not in any way, if I can help it.'

'Nathan. I get that. In spades. Otherwise we wouldn't have been spending as much time together as we have. Even though it's only been a short time, I trust you. It's me who hasn't been up-front about everything.' Her breasts rose and the last drop of colour drained from her face. 'I don't see me having babies any time soon. If at all. And they're important to you.'

His heart slowed, his lungs seized, his head spun, yet his eyes never left hers as he tried to figure out where this was going. 'You said you wanted kids.'

'Yes. One day, maybe. Right now I'm getting back on my feet after the horror that was my marriage. I don't know what I want for the future. I don't trust myself to get it right straight away. It's too soon.'

'I understand that.' As much as he could, because it was a bit like him falling in love with her after the wonderful relationship he'd had with Rosie. But he hadn't known fear like Molly had. Hadn't had his belief in Rosie undermined. Hadn't seen those she should've been able to trust not back her until later on, by which time her heart had already been broken. So, really, he knew nothing about where Molly was coming from.

Suddenly she was right in front of him, hands gripping hips, her eyes flashing. 'No, you don't,' she yelled.

Nathan waited, not wanting to risk upsetting her further.

She breathed deeply, said in a quieter voice, 'I

know you've tried, but I'm still working at understanding myself, so how can you?'

He began to rise, to scoop her into his arms and hold her safe.

Her hand shot up in the stop sign again. 'No. Please, no.'

He stilled, waited.

'Sit down. Please,' she added quietly, and he knew she hadn't finished. In fact, she started before he'd taken a step, like it was a force that had to be set free. 'Watching you with your family brought it home to me that I'm being unfair to expect you to spend time with me when I can't guarantee I'll ever be ready to want to settle down, let alone have a family. If we could guarantee we'd have some fun and walk away happy then...'

She swallowed hard. 'I'm screwed up, Nathan, and while I might have stopped looking over my shoulder at every turn, I still have nightmares about being strong enough to cope with what's ahead.'

'You're stronger than anyone I know,' he ground out through the anger filling him for the man who'd done this to sweet, beautiful Molly.

'It's skin deep,' she whispered. 'Those steps I talk about taking—a toddler could do better.'

'You're taking them. That's all that matters.' Still he wanted to haul her into his arms and never let her go, to make her feel better, and stop the ache that was expanding in his chest. But the stop sign was still in her eyes, in the tight way she held herself, as though if she relaxed even a fraction she'd shatter. He also wanted, needed, to fight her gremlins for her, but Molly would never let him do that. She fought her own battles. All he could do was be there for her. 'You need more time. We don't have to stop seeing each other.'

'And if I still don't feel I can have a permanent relationship after we've spent a lot of time together?' Her curls shook as she talked. 'No, Nathan. You deserve better than that. You can love again, and have the life you want. You've been honest about your love of family and the children you want one day. I will not risk taking that opportunity away from you.'

Yeah, the news was starting to seep in around the edges of the haze in his mind, and making him begin to understand the full impact of what Molly was telling him. He had always wanted children. Growing up in a large, happy family, it had been a given he'd add to the clan, as his sisters had. Not once, not even when Rosie had died, had he given up on that dream completely. But did he want them at the cost of love? He was half in love with Molly already. Half? Now was not the time to think about it. He'd finally let a woman close for the first time since Rosie. Yeah, and look where that was getting him.

His heart was on the way to taking another battering. He didn't want to lose Molly, he wanted them to make this journey together. If at the end of it she still wasn't ready for him then he'd have to take it on the chin. But he wanted the opportunity to give it all he had. 'Why haven't you said any of this earlier?' It might've saved him falling for her. Except he'd thought that had begun the day she'd started in the department. 'You've told me so much about what happened, it would've been simple to finish it with this. I'd at least have been warned.' Anger was beginning to simmer. At her for not trusting him enough, at himself for falling for her, for finally letting go the restraints Rosie's death had put on his heart.

'At first I didn't see what was happening. I do want love and family. One day. If I can get past all that's happened. I'm afraid I might be reading too much into my feelings for you. You're everything Paul wasn't. I want that. What I don't want is to make you into someone you're not, and I could be unwittingly doing that. I need time, and getting out and about with people, before I'm ready for a commitment. It's essential to know I'm not making another horrendous mistake—for everyone's sake.'

Pain sifted through his tight chest muscles. This was not how he'd seen the night finishing. But life loved throwing curveballs. He already knew that, had dealt with it and had thought he was coming out the other side.

'I'll always be here for you, Molly. I care a lot about you.' Damn it. He wanted to say he'd move on and be grateful she'd thought of him when trying to sort her life out, but he couldn't. It wasn't true. Neither was telling her he was falling in love with her a wise idea. It'd be putting everything back on her, and it was obvious she already felt terrible about this. He also had to own some of it for rushing in.

'You sure we can't continue as we are, and see how it turns out?' He wouldn't get down on bended knee. Only because he already knew it wouldn't work and he had to have some pride left when she walked out.

Knuckling her eyes, she took her time answering him. 'I'm sorry. I didn't know if we were having a couple of dates and then getting back to life as it used to be, though a lot friendlier, or we'd end up disliking each other.'

'Stop saying sorry. You're being truthful.'

'And that includes being sorry.' She shook her head, those blasted curls flicking in every direction. 'I wanted another week with you before I said what was bothering me.' She swallowed. 'I once believed in love so much I thought it could overcome everything, now it's hard to accept I was wrong.'

So she'd been happy with him. That put the final wedge in the situation. Molly O'Keefe had wanted to spend more time with him and she'd just made absolutely certain it wasn't going to happen.

Molly staggered into her apartment and sank to the floor. She'd lied to Nathan—again by omission, but she'd been untruthful all the same. He deserved better. Through what Paul had done to her, she'd become someone else, a person she barely recognised at times. Honesty was of paramount importance now. On the other hand, telling Nathan about the small chance she'd ever get pregnant wasn't ever going to happen. If he'd said he'd take the risk, she'd have to live with the hurt caused if it didn't happen. She was not prepared to do that. He'd thank her one day.

Her heart was shredding, her head throwing so many accusations at her about dumping Nathan, it was a wonder she'd managed to drive home safely from Coogee. But she had. There wasn't anywhere else for her to be. This was her home—small, lonely, but hers. She did not belong in Nathan's house, or in his flat.

How had she fallen in love so quickly? The

answer didn't matter. She did love Nathan. Though what she'd told him was also true. It might only be a step in getting her life back. A temporary one, though judging by the agony in her chest that was complete and utter nonsense. With Paul she'd believed love would win the day. How wrong could she have been? That was the reason she was struggling to believe in herself now.

Yet, deep inside, a kernel of hope and longing and that love said this was for real. That Nathan was the right man for her. He'd always look out for her, come what may.

'I did the right thing. Especially for Nathan.' *Didn't I?*

'Yes.'

She had to believe this was the right way to go or she'd never get up in the morning. But, hell, she hurt. Everywhere. Who'd have thought she'd feel like this after such a short time with Nathan? Truthfully? She'd never expected to fall in love again when Paul had blotted her thoughts of what love was meant to be. But she had. And thereby done the right thing by Nathan in walking away before they got in too deep. Except she'd already done that. Deep, then deeper, her heart was tied up in knots for him.

Her phone lit up as a text came in. You get home all right? Nathan. Caring to the end.

A waterfall cascaded down her cheeks. Something special and wonderful had ended. She had to be that strong woman he mistakenly believed she was. Fake it till she made it.

Tap, tap on the phone. Yes. Sorry. Molly paused. Stop saying sorry. She deleted the word, typed, Thanks, and pushed Send. *Fake it*.

Her bed was cold—and lonely.

Her head ached. The pillow was soon soaked.

Her heart went through the act of giving her life, all excitement and happiness gone, just a regular pumping.

So much for finally joining in on the work social scene. She'd been afraid of trusting people and had been the one to dump on Nathan's trust. Now she had to continue working with him because running away was not an option. She'd stand tall and take the knocks. *And* be strong, even if she had to fake it in the beginning.

Until now she'd believed of all the things Paul had done, taking away her baby and leaving her with only one damaged Fallopian tube was the hardest thing to deal with. Now she knew different. Walking away from Nathan was worse. He'd lost Rosie; he didn't need to lose his chance of having children with someone in the future. His nieces and nephews adored him, and the youngsters he dealt with in the ED were always in awe of him. He'd be an amazing father.

Snatching the box of tissues, she scrubbed her face, but still the tears flowed. Never before had the knowledge of not being able to have a child been quite so devastating. No children, no Nathan.

CHAPTER ELEVEN

'CAN YOU LOOK at two-year-old Lucy Charles?' Molly asked Nathan. 'She's got a plastic top from a small tube stuck in her ear. She's a right little cutie, even if she is screaming the place down.'

'You've tried oil to get the top out?' Nathan asked, ever the professional with her, though there were times he'd ask how she was doing at basketball or in the op shop.

Over the past month she'd become so used to the thudding in her chest whenever she was near him that she could answer without hesitation now. 'No. She's not letting anyone near her head, let alone the offending ear.' Maybe Nathan could charm the wee dot into letting him make her better.

'It's never easy with a toddler.' Nathan swung open the curtain to the cubicle from which shrieks emanated. 'Hello, Mrs Charles. I'm Nathan, a doctor.' He crouched down to be face to face with the little girl. 'Hey, Lucy. What's that on your shirt?' He pointed to the rabbit.

Lucy stared at him, hiccupping through her tears.

'Is it a cat?'

A headshake.

'Is it a horse?'

Another shake.

Nathan put his finger to his lips. 'I don't know, then. You'll have to tell me.'

'Wabbit.'

'So it is. Have you named it?'

'Wobby.'

'Can I look at his ear? It's so big.'

Lucy stared at him, then looked at her mother.

'Go on, show the doctor Robby's ear.'

Without touching her T-shirt, Nathan pointed to the rabbit's ear. 'Look, there's something stuck in there. I'm going to have to pull it out.' Clenching his hand tight, still without touching the shirt, he made a pulling motion and then looked into his palm. 'Yes, I've got it. Wobby didn't feel a thing. Now can I see your ear?'

Lucy shook her head.

'Not easily tricked, are you, little one?' To Lucy's mother, he said, 'I'm going to give her something to quieten her down enough so I can remove the obstruction. She'll be sleepy for an hour or two afterwards but there won't be any side effects.' Then he said to Molly, 'Can you get the drugs? I don't want to leave Lucy while she's comfortable with me.'

'Sure.' Nathan was so good with kids. Her heart skittered. She knew that. It was why she'd walked away from him, but it wasn't getting any easier to accept. Seeing him every day in the department, she was constantly questioning her ability to carry on working here. But she had to. She'd vowed not to weaken, to be that strong woman Nathan believed she was.

Once Lucy accepted the syrup she began to calm down almost immediately and the button was soon removed, then she was on her way home with her mother, and Molly went looking for someone else to help.

'Molly, ready for a break?' Vicki appeared around a corner.

'Is it time already?' She had no appetite for the soup she'd brought from the local deli but she'd go through the motions. Changing direction, she headed for her locker.

'Sure is. You were miles away. Or maybe only three cubicles down, where a certain doctor is about to examine an abscess.'

'You got nothing better to do than make up stuff?' Molly asked around the longing that wasn't in a hurry to go away.

'Better than thinking about my own problems.'

'You heard from Cole today?'

'Four times. They're heading back to Randwick late Saturday.'

Molly smiled as she opened her locker to retrieve her supper. 'That's good news.'

'It is.'

That's it? Not sure whether to press for more, Molly stayed quiet. As her soup heated in the microwave she threw out, 'You know where I am. Come round for coffee any time.'

'What time are we going to look at that apartment?'

'Eleven tomorrow morning.'

'I might watch your basketball game too.' Vicki wasn't getting her nails done, or sprucing up the apartment for Cole? There was definitely something wrong.

Molly shivered. She and her new friend made a right sorry pair.

Nathan held his breath. What apartment? Where? Molly was moving? His flat was still available.

Yes, but she doesn't want you in her life outside here.

He should be glad Vicki was going with her to check out the new place, but all he could think was, *Why didn't you ask me to go along?*

Making an abrupt turn, he headed for the lift to go downstairs to the cafeteria. Sitting in the same small room with Molly, hearing her talking and laughing with others, was too much.

She didn't ignore him at work, did her best to remain friendly and approachable without expecting any special attention, which he'd had to back off from giving or risk upsetting her further. Yet it was as though she was a stranger. Wound up in plastic wrap, visible yet unavailable, nothing changing. His life was on hold. His head spun.

Life could be horrid, throw up the worst of bad deals, and Molly had had more than her fair share. He hurt with missing her. But he also had to sort out what it was he wanted in life. For all Molly had said, she was right about one thing. He did want a family. But he wanted it with her. Which it seemed was an impossibility, for now at least.

Then again, the day would probably come when Molly was ready, and then what? If he'd walked away as she was trying to make him do then they'd have missed out on the wonderful, loving relationship that he believed was possible. The question he'd been asking himself for the past weeks was, *Do I want to miss out on love so I can have children?*

The only answer that made its way into his

skull was no. Yet he hesitated to try and persuade Molly to take a chance on them. Something in the pain that had bored into him from her desperate eyes when she'd told him she might be making a mistake held him back. *He* didn't want to cause *her* any more pain.

His phone rang. 'You're lucky I'm taking a break,' he told his sister. 'You working late?' It was after midnight.

'Only time it's quiet around here.'

'The joy of having those brats.'

'We're not coming up for the weekend,' Allie said. 'Russ has pulled a murder inquiry.'

'You and the kids can still come down.'

'Or you and Molly could come here for the weekend.'

It was like a punch in the gut. His sister thought Molly was a serious part of his life. 'She's got other things on.'

'Nathan, you've let her get away, haven't you?'

'You've read too much into our relationship.'

'We all think she's wonderful. She fitted in with everyone, and that's saying something.'

How true. 'You're right on that score.' Why did Allie automatically think he was at fault for Molly no longer being on the scene?

Ever consider Molly might have dumped me?

'I'm going now. I need to eat before I get hauled back to the department for someone who had nothing better to do on a Friday night than get into a scrap somewhere.'

'Nathan.'

'If I didn't know better, I'd say that was Mum talking to me.'

Allie chuckled. 'Believe it, brother. Now, tell me what's going on.'

'I'm at work, Allie.'

'Having a break. You wouldn't be worrying what Rosie would have to say about you finding someone else, by any chance?'

'Hardly. She told me to move on and not live on my own for ever.' So why the hesitation on his part? He couldn't put it all on Molly. Was trying to save her pain an excuse for his own insecurities? Talk about mixed up. At some point they both had to take a step into the unknown, whether it was together or with other people. He wanted to do it with Molly. So *was* he worried about letting Rosie's memory down?

'Are you sure?' His sister echoed his doubts.

No, he wasn't sure about any damned thing. 'Got to go. Talk later in the week.' He ended the call before Allie said anything else disruptive to his thinking. Not that it was hard to do, he thought as he bit into the chicken roll he'd bought at his favourite bakery. Today they'd failed him. The roll was tasteless, the bread dry, and there wasn't enough mayo. Tipping the lukewarm coffee down the sink, he went back to work in search of a distraction. One that didn't have red curls and sad eyes.

Saturday morning found Nathan charging up and down the lawn with the mower as if a swarm of bees was after him. How was Molly's apartment viewing going? The place was closer to Bondi Beach than Bondi Junction. She'd shown no reticence about filling him in on the scant details she'd obtained from the agency when he'd asked. He hadn't asked what had happened to the idea of purchasing a property. Could be she wasn't as ready for something permanent after all. It's what she'd said about a relationship with him.

Nathan ran out of lawn to do battle with. Now what? If there were some waves he'd go surfing, but the sea couldn't be calmer. If only the kids had turned up. He was in his happy zone with them. Family was what it was all about.

There's more to family than just the children. You need the right woman first. Not only as the mother but for you, your partner, lover, holder of your heart.

He shook his head. When he'd finally found the woman he wanted to be with, a woman he'd started letting into his heart, it had all gone wrong.

Did I scare her off?

Nathan sank down on one of the outdoor stools and stared unseeingly out to sea. Was that why she'd pulled out? The only thing wrong with that idea was that she'd sounded so genuine about not being sure of herself, of needing more time to become comfortable with herself. A lot more comfortable. Molly didn't lie or exaggerate. She'd meant every word, so he could relax on that score. He hadn't frightened her away. But there had been more to what she'd said. He'd seen it flicker through her eyes as she'd turned to leave that night.

Could it be his need to have children that was the problem? That she was afraid of letting him down? Because she would be nervous about not getting everything right with the man she finally gave her heart to. That was a given, after what her ex had done to her.

This was getting too complicated. Overthinking everything in an attempt to find answers that only Molly could give him.

Tugging his phone from his pocket, he called Molly on speed dial, and listened to the ringing go on and on until voice mail picked up. Hearing her message to leave a number and name made his heart slow and his stomach tighten. Damn it. After Rosie had died he'd often rung her phone just to hear her voice. He hit 'end'. This was spooky. Molly was out there somewhere. He'd see her on Monday if not before. She hadn't gone away for ever. Comparing the situation with that of Rosie was desperate.

He rang Molly's number again. 'Hey, Molly, it's Nathan. Give me a buzz when you get a moment. Nothing urgent.'

She must've got that because he didn't hear back from her.

Finally, unable to focus on any of the chores that needed doing, he went for a drive. It wasn't until he was driving over the Harbour Bridge that he realised where he was going. A calm settled over him. Yes, he needed to do this, to find out if he was ready to move forward.

The house was small, tired, and didn't touch him in any way. Rosie's immaculate gardens were a riot of weeds and kids' toys, and he felt a moment of sadness for what had been. A dog lay on the front porch, too lazy to lift its head when he stopped at the front gate. He and Rosie had intended getting a dog one day when there was time to look after it properly, but seeing the setter sprawled over the spot Rosie had used to sit in the sun didn't raise any feeling other than nostalgia.

'I miss you, darling, but you've gone. As has the house with all our hopes and dreams. It's someone else's paradise now.' Like Rosie, it had morphed into something different, freeing him to get on with his life, to make a new future with Molly. He'd always miss Rosie, love her quietly, but to spend for ever mourning her was to waste the life he'd been given. As Rosie had told him in that last hideous week, 'Life's precious, Nat. Grab it and make the most of what you get. Don't spend it all thinking about what might've been. Do it for me, if not yourself.'

'Actually, Rosie, I am going to do this for me. And Molly.' There was a spring in his step as he walked away from the past.

The band was so loud her eardrums were bursting. It was also out of tune and the guy at the microphone couldn't have sung his way out of a paper bag if he'd tried.

'That's terrible.' Molly grimaced, and took a sip of her vodka. The second in one night. *Turning into a lush, girl.*

Vicki raised her glass in salute. 'At least he's still upright, unlike the drummer.'

They were at a bar in Randwick, close to the army base. Needing to be busy, Molly had offered to drive Vicki out here to meet Cole when his unit got into town early in the morning. After checking into a motel down the road, they'd come along to the pub for a meal, though Molly had barely touched her food, her stomach permanently tied in knots. Her clothes were a little looser too. Funny how once she'd have been thrilled about that, and now thought she looked better with a little weight on her hips to fill out her gorgeous trousers and skirts.

Molly looked around at the crowd and wished she'd stayed in the city. She didn't belong here. Standing up, she set her half-full glass aside. 'Let's go. I can't take any more of this.'

'Spoilsport.' But Vicki was quick to follow her. Outside they both checked their phones. Vicki scowled. 'Nothing. Where's Cole?'

Molly stared at her screen. 'One missed call.' She knew the number off by heart. 'Nathan.' They still talked, although not in a relaxed way as before. He hadn't phoned her since they'd gone their separate ways. If he hadn't said it wasn't urgent, she'd be starting to worry.

'What did he want?'

Molly shrugged. 'No idea.' She'd love to talk to him, to touch his hand, and feel his lips on her cheek. It wasn't going to happen. She'd left him. It was over.

'Here we are.' Vicki gestured to the bright neon lights flickering on and off. 'Why are we staying in a motel when I could be at home in my big comfy bed, watching TV?'

'Because Cole is about to ride into town, looking for you,' Molly said. 'Plus I don't drive after drinking.' Neither did she want to go home to her empty apartment. It echoed of Nathan. Fingers crossed, she'd be moving very soon. The owner of the place she'd inspected that morning was getting back to her tomorrow after he'd checked exactly when the current tenants were moving out. She hadn't found the strength to go looking for somewhere to buy. Seemed she wasn't as far ahead in her new life as she'd hoped.

Right then Vicki got a text. 'Cole says he'll be knocking down the door at six.'

'I'll get out of the way by a quarter to.' Molly set the alarm on her phone.

'Don't rush off on my account. Damned time of the month. The army never gets it right.'

She grinned. 'Some things we can't control. But I still don't want to be here for the reunion.' Molly stripped down to her underwear and slid under the covers of the nearest bed. 'Get some sleep so you're not dozing off on your husband.'

Molly fell asleep immediately, only to sit bolt upright some time later, her head thumping along with her heart. Time of the month. No. Not possible. Can't be. Picking up her phone, she brought up the calendar.

Closing her eyes, she drew air into her lungs, and tried again. It had been due last week. Her periods were never reliable. This would be another example of nature rubbing her loss in her face. But—what if… No. She tossed the duvet aside and clambered out of bed to sit on the hard chair, her legs tucked under her, her body trembling. Sleep would be impossible. At least until she found out if she was pregnant.

She *couldn't* be.

She showered, dressed, and crept out of the unit at five thirty, leaving a note saying, 'Have a great couple of days. See you at work.'

In the car with the engine running she blew on her cold hands. Now what? It was too early for any shops to be open to buy a test kit. But she wanted to be at home when she found out the result so headed for Bondi Junction, concentrating on driving and not what she'd do if the test was positive. Go knock on Nathan's door and apologise for walking away from him so quickly?

What had to happen was that she did not make any rushed, emotionally driven decisions that she'd come to regret.

Damn it. Her hand hurt where she'd hit the steering wheel. This was crazy. Here she was already thinking the test would be positive when in all reality there'd be no blue line. Her stomach sank. The gynaecologist had been clear about her slight chance of having a baby.

In Bondi Junction she sat outside the shopping centre, feeling ill, until it opened. With her purchase finally in her hand, she headed for home and privacy, afraid of the outcome, almost too scared to find out. Almost.

'Answer your damned phone, Molly O'Keefe,' Nathan shouted, dropping his on the bench with a clatter. 'I need to talk to you,' he added in a lower tone. 'Please.'

He paced the kitchen. Think of another way to get her attention. Climb the Harbour Bridge and threaten to jump off? Then she'd really believe he was mad. Mad for her might not work in the circumstances.

The phone rang. Hope soared. Allie's name blinked at him. Not in the mood for her wisecracks or helpful suggestions, he ignored her. She'd told him the family thought Molly was the bee's knees. His gut had been telling him the same for weeks now. If only he'd listened earlier he might not be feeling so sore and uptight.

He did need to talk to someone, just not his sister. Molly. Snatching up the keys to his four-wheel drive, he headed for the garage, where he paused. If she wasn't taking his calls then what were the chances she'd let him into her apartment? His gaze fell on the monster car, the sparkling paintwork reminding him it hadn't been out for a run in weeks. Not since the day he'd brought Molly home for the first time. The day he'd suggested a fast ride out of the city. The first time he'd seen how excitement turned her eyes to emeralds and brought tenderness to her face.

Now he knew what to do. His finger zipped across the keys on his phone.

Hey, Molly, feel up to that ride in the red machine I promised weeks ago? I'm heading for the Blue Mountains and would like some company.

He pushed Send before he had time to overthink things. Now what? Stand here waiting for a reply that most likely wasn't coming? Nope. He'd pack a picnic, find a blanket to spread on the grass, and put a bottle of wine in a chiller pack. Then he'd change into something less manky and head for Bondi Junction.

Midmorning, Molly gave up on her walk and let herself into the apartment, automatically reaching for the kettle to make tea. Her stomach told her it was not taking tea or anything else right at the moment. But she needed to eat. She had a baby on board to look out for. She also needed sleep, but that was probably asking too much when she felt wired. And with her mind throwing up so many questions and doubts—all to do with Nathan. The father of her baby. He had to be told, and soon. She wouldn't hold out on him. This new version of herself—still tinged with the old one but getting past that—would not hold back on the truth. All of it this time.

Her phone pinged. Nathan again.

Hey, Molly, feel up to that ride in the red machine I promised weeks ago? I'm heading for the Blue Mountains and would like some company.

So would I. Yours especially.

But would Nathan still be talking to her after she gave him her news? Or would he say she'd only told him to get back with him for all the wrong reasons? Only one way to find out. Shirking this was what the old Molly would've done. She was going to be a mother; she had to be tougher than she'd ever been. Starting with talking straight to Nathan.

Sinking onto a chair, she stared at the phone in her shaky hand. *Do it.*

Yes, please. Then she dug deeper. Do I get to drive?

I promised, didn't I? Ten minutes away.

Ten minutes? What was she going to wear? The most important date of her life and she had to look good. Sensational even. She was going to blow Nathan out of the water with her news and—and he wouldn't care about what she was wearing. Her shoulders dropped.

This is being tough?

The green floral dress was too loose, the black trousers and orange shirt didn't go with the new boots, the red blouse and cream trousers looked good and felt all wrong. The pile on the floor grew as her wardrobe emptied.

'What will you think of me when I tell you the rest of why I had to leave you, eh, Nathan?'

Ding-dong.

She was about to find out. Unless— No, she was not going to chicken out.

Ding-dong.

Molly ran through the apartment in her underwear and stabbed the button by the door. 'You can't come up. I'll be with you shortly.' Not waiting for his reply, she raced back to her bedroom and tugged on jeans and pulled a cream jersey over her head. But when her curls refused to be contained she stopped to stare at herself in the mirror.

What do I care about my appearance? We're going for a drive and I'm going to tell him about the baby and then he'll bring me home and life will go on as it has for the past few weeks.

Picking up a twist tie, she bundled up her hair and aimed for the door, not bothering with make-up. There'd be no drive anywhere. She couldn't sit beside Nathan pretending all was well in her world on the trip to the Blue Mountains.

Nathan was leaning against his fancy car, his arms crossed over his chest, his eyes fixed on her from the moment she stepped outside. 'Molly, I've missed you.'

She didn't bother with the rejoinder about seeing each other every day at work. They both knew that's not what he meant. Her mouth flattened. Where to start?

He continued, 'You look pale, and those shadows under your eyes are a worry.'

She stared at the man she loved, the man she was about to rock off his pedestal. 'You're not looking so perky yourself.' Then she looked harder. Wrong, Mol. There was something assured about him, a confidence— No, Nathan was always confident. Today he looked comfortable in his own skin. 'Forget I said that. You look great.' Might as well start out as she meant to go on.

'You think? I've not been sleeping very well.'

'Me neither.' Nights spent tossing and turning, trying to solve the riddle that was her life.

Come on, get this over. Before we get into the car, and then I won't have an agonising hour on the road sitting beside him as he takes in what I have to say.

The words stuck in her throat, refused to budge.

'Come on. Let's get on the road.' He held the driver's door open for her.

Finally she managed to speak. 'Nathan, I've got things to tell you first.'

'Same. But let's not do it out on the street. I'd like to take you to the mountains where we can talk all day if necessary. Please.'

The trip home afterwards might be long and cold. Or—or it might be the greatest trip she'd ever made. It might also be her last time with him. 'Okay. But you drive.' She wouldn't be focused enough.

'Now you're worrying me.'

There was a small smile coming her way and she ran with it, gave a tight one back. 'Let's go.'

They rode in silence, tension building as the kilometres flew by. At one point Molly wanted it over, then she wanted to continue driving the highway right into the night.

Nathan finally pulled into a parking area and turned off the engine. 'Want to walk a bit?'

'Yes.' It would be easier saying what was bottled up inside her if she was moving, not sitting looking directly at Nathan. But when he took her hand as they strolled along a path heading out to a bush-clad hillside, she nearly cried. She'd missed his touch. Face it, she'd missed everything that was Nathan. Even his grumpiness, though there had been some of that at intense moments in the department.

'Molly, I've screwed up big-time.'

Hello? She tried to pull her hand free, but he tightened his grip.

'Hear me out, please?'

'Nathan, there are things you need know first.' Panic started squeezing her chest. 'I haven't been entirely honest with you.'

'Stop, Molly. I could say the same.'

What? Nathan was so honest it could be brutal. Or was that wishful thinking? By hoping for the man of her dreams to push away the past, had she overlooked his faults? No. She wouldn't believe that for a moment. This was the man she trusted completely, did not expect to turn into a monster once she'd given him her heart. 'Go on.'

He stopped walking and turned to face her, reached for her other hand. 'I love you. I think I have from the first time I set eyes on you.'

Her knees sagged. This was not what she had been expecting. Not that she knew what he'd been going to say, but it sure hadn't been this. 'I—'

He shook his head. 'Let me finish. Yes, I love you with all my heart. But I don't want to rush you into anything you're not ready for. I hear your uncertainty about being ready for a relationship. I'll wait for you, Mol, for as long as it takes.' He swallowed, tightened his hold on her hands. 'And if you decide I'm not the man for you then I'll deal with that too.'

Tears spurted down her face. Nathan loved her. The man she'd fallen for loved her. They could make this work. Be a family. She could forget the past, be happy again. Tell him first she loved him? Or about the baby? He mustn't think her love was because of the baby, and that she needed him onside for that only. 'I'm pregnant.'

'What?' He rocked forward like he'd taken a blow to the solar plexus. 'You're—*we're*—pregnant?'

'Yes.' She stepped back, tugging free of his grip. And he let her go. 'I don't know how it happened as we were always careful, and my chances of getting pregnant were slim.'

'We didn't use protection that first time. Besides, those condoms had been lying in my drawer for a while. Hang on. Why were your chances slim?' Then understanding dawned in his eyes, tightened his mouth. 'That scar on your tummy. He did that, didn't he?'

She nodded. 'I was four months along. Paul was jealous of our unborn baby. Said he wasn't sharing me with anyone, not even his own child.'

'Oh, Mol.' As Nathan wound her into his

arms, he asked, 'Has that got anything to do with why you said you couldn't go on seeing me?'

Leaning back to read his expression, she nodded. 'I've only got one Fallopian tube, and even that's not in the best shape for conception. Or so the specialist thought. It seems he was wrong.' Nothing showing in Nathan's face said she shouldn't continue. 'You want a family, I couldn't guarantee you one, so in a way I lied. I didn't want to hurt you in the future when a baby didn't come along. If I'd told you, you might've felt sorry for me and pretended everything was all right.'

'I'd never do that.'

She nodded. 'Deep down I knew it, but I'm still insecure about knowing I'm right when it comes to understanding you. But I know for certain my love for you is real, and everlasting.'

'You love me?' A smile that was pure Nathan split his face, and melted the last band around her heart. For the first time in years she relaxed totally. 'You love me.' His hands were on her waist, lifting her, and then they were spinning in a circle. 'And I love you. That's all that matters.'

He believed her—he didn't think she'd said it because she needed a father for her baby. There was so much happiness in his face she knew he meant what he'd said. 'It is. You make me whole again,' she whispered, just before his mouth claimed hers.

Then he stopped. Pulled back, still holding her. 'Molly, please say you'll marry me. I promise to love you for ever and ever.'

'Yes, Nathan, I will. Because you love me. Not because of the baby.' That she'd have on her own if he didn't love her. But he did. He'd said so, and Nathan always told the truth.

'Yes, Mol, I do, with all my being and then some. And I love the baby already.'

The next kiss rolled into another and then another, and turned them towards the car and the picnic and the blanket. Especially the blanket and the thick bush not too far away.

Six weeks later

'I pronounce you man and wife,' announced the marriage celebrant. 'Nathan, you may kiss the bride.'

The house rocked with laughter and cheers as family and friends, dressed to the nines, crowded round.

'That's enough. Some of us have only got the weekend off.' Cole nudged Nathan when the kiss went on for ever.

Nathan came up for air and gave his mate a

glare. 'Thank goodness for that. I couldn't put up with your crassness for any longer.'

Molly grinned as she shook her head at them. 'Boys, stop it.'

Cole hauled her in for a big hug. 'I'm so glad he found you.'

'So am I,' Molly admitted, sudden tears threatening.

'He didn't find her, I pushed them together.' Vicki grinned.

'Here, you're soaking your dress.' Nathan handed her a handkerchief.

Molly laughed. 'Who has these any more?' She carefully wiped her eyes, aware of not messing her make-up, done by a woman Vicki had hired from the cosmetic department of one of Sydney's large stores for them and Lizzie.

'You want me to produce a handful of tissues instead?' her husband asked.

Her husband. She pinched herself. No, she wasn't dreaming. This was real. She'd found love again, this time with the right man. Hadn't had to fake a thing. Looking at him as he waved to the waiter with a tray of champagne glasses, her heart swelled till it hurt. Damn, but she was so lucky.

'Molly Lupton, you lucky girl.' Lizzie swept her into a hug. 'I am so happy for you.'

'I glad you made it in time.'

Lizzie gave an awkward laugh. 'Well, you know me. Stubborn to the end.'

'You won't lose your job because you've taken these few days off?' She'd been working on intense negotiations in Hong Kong until two days ago.

'Let them try. I might be the only person to come from Perth, but I'm the best.'

Molly hugged her friend. 'You are so right.'

'Your mum's thrilled, by the way.'

Molly looked across the lawn to where her parents and Dad's new lady stood together, watching the proceedings, as though unsure how welcome they were. 'I know, and this time when she says she likes my husband I'm going to accept that. We both made mistakes, and I don't want those to ruin the future. My babies need their grandparents to be there for them like Gran was for me.'

'Babies? As in plural?' Nathan had appeared beside her, two glasses of champagne in one hand.

She stretched up on the tips of her beautiful, pointy cream shoes and whispered, 'Twins.'

He shoved the glasses at Lizzie, reached for Molly and spun her around and up into his arms. 'Twins,' he yelled. 'We're having two little blighters, not one.'

So much for keeping the pregnancy quiet until

they got through the first trimester and well into the second. Clapping and cheeky comments exploded around them, glasses were raised, and finally Molly got one of her own to take, not one or two, but three small sips from before putting it aside. No more for her until the babies were born. 'My husband, baby one and baby two. I love you all.'

And months later:

Nathan rushed through the Saturday afternoon crowd, elbowing people out of his way. Typical bloody weekend. Everyone was getting out amongst it, and in his way.

The ED had been flat out, dealing with idiots who'd had too much food and alcohol when he'd got the call to go to the maternity unit. Molly had gone into labour at thirty-five weeks. It had been fast, almost too much so, but the babies were in good shape, tiny and absolutely beautiful. Like their mother.

Two teddy bears and one enormous bunch of irises was a lot to protect from these idiots who weren't looking where they were going, but at last the main entrance to the hospital loomed up in his line of vision. Why the hospital gift shop had to be closed today of all days he didn't know.

The lift was slow to arrive, and when it came,

people surged past him to fill it to capacity. 'Typical,' he muttered as he charged up the stairs, reaching the maternity floor out of breath and having to bend over double while his lungs recovered.

Then he was racing down the corridor, out of breath for a different reason. Excitement gripped him, and his face ached as his smile knew no boundaries. 'I'm a dad, I'm a dad.' Spinning into Molly's room, he rushed up to the bed to hug her, forgetting he had his arms full. Slamming on the brakes, he swallowed. Both babies were snuggled against her breasts, eyes closed, cute little pink noses. He couldn't hug her anyway. 'I'm married to the most wonderful woman on the planet. Mrs-Beautiful-Molly-Mother-of-Two-Lupton.'

'Glad you remembered.' Molly laughed tiredly. 'Want to hold someone?'

'Yes, you.' He placed the teddies on the only chair and held out the flowers. 'I bought every last Dutch iris in the shop.'

'Did you get some vases? There's only one jar in here.' She was grinning at him now, sending his stomach into a riot of longing and happiness.

Damn, he loved this woman so much. His son and daughter were a bonus. It was Molly he woke up for every day. 'I love you, Molly Lupton.'

She nodded. 'I know. Love you back. Now, about names.'

That was an ongoing debate. Hopefully they'd have it sorted by the time everyone went home. Tomorrow.

Tomorrow.

'Joshua and Karina?'

Molly nodded, a look of glee at having won the battle on her face. 'Joshua and Karina.'

How could he refuse her anything?

* * * * *

*If you enjoyed this story, check out
these other great reads from
Sue MacKay*

Taking a Chance on the Single Dad
Redeeming Her Brooding Surgeon
The Italian Surgeon's Secret Baby
ER Doc's Forever Gift

All available now!